## "You will marry me," Tyler stated flatly

Kate's eyes widened. "You can't be serious. You can't possibly want to marry me. You don't even like me!"

"That's beside the point. I want control of Langston Industries and you want control of your life. To gain these ends we have to marry and stay together for two years. Also, we have to convince my father we're trying to make our marriage work. That will mean we will have to share a bed...and I am not a celibate sort of man."

Tyler paused, then asked, "Do we have an agreement?"

Kate's stomach churned. To Tyler she was only a piece of merchandise, bought to fulfill his father's demand.

But what choice had she? The alternative was too horrible to contemplate.

"Yes," she said at last, "we have an agreement...."

**BETSY PAGE**, an American author, decided to write her first book when she was pregnant with her third son. She was reading a romance novel and found herself saying, "My heroine would have more spunk." Now she can't imagine a better occupation, one that allows her to stay home with the children—something she strongly believes in—and spend her days fantasizing about heroes and heroines. And she stresses how lucky she is to have a very supportive husband.

## Books by Betsy Page

Don't miss any of our special offers. Write to us at the following address for information on our newest releases.

Harlequin Reader Service
901 Fuhrmann Blvd., P.O. Box 1397, Buffalo, NY 14240
Canadian address: P.O. Box 603,
Fort Erie, Ont. L2A 5X3

# BETSY PAGE

## the arrangement

*Harlequin Books*

TORONTO • NEW YORK • LONDON
AMSTERDAM • PARIS • SYDNEY • HAMBURG
STOCKHOLM • ATHENS • TOKYO • MILAN

Harlequin Presents first edition March 1987
ISBN 0-373-10965-2

# CHAPTER ONE

"YOU CAN'T BE SERIOUS!"

Tyler Langston was incredulous. Lines of stress created by the running of Tyler Industries gave character to a face that was ruggedly handsome. His movements, as his agitated strides carried him back and forth across the room in rapid succession, gave evidence of physical prowess. He was not a man accustomed to being dictated to. He was accustomed to doing the dictating, and his actions were not unlike those of a wild animal suddenly finding itself being drawn into a trap.

"You're giving me whiplash," an older version of Tyler complained from behind a large carved oak desk as he was forced to turn his head from side to side in order to follow his son's angry pacing. His hair was white in contrast to the dark brown of the younger man's, but his eyes were just as brown and just as sharp. "And I am serious."

"Arranged marriages are archaic." Tyler came to a halt in front of the desk. There was an authority in his bearing that intimidated most people.

Even Uriah Langston had to admit that he felt a certain uneasiness, but his mind was made up. "Arranged marriages are still practiced in some very civilized alcoves of society, and considering your sister's disastrous failures, the practice is beginning to look better and better to me by the moment. However, I am not arranging the marriage. I am merely telling you who I want you to marry."

Leaning forward on the desk, his palms flat on the surface, Tyler faced his father and said tersely, "I will find a wife in my own good time, and I will decide when I want to marry."

"You've gone through a string of mistresses, not one of whom would make a decent wife." Uriah shook his head.

"I've been too busy running this company to scour the hills looking for good sturdy pioneer stock," Tyler countered hotly.

"Precisely!" His father smiled triumphantly. "So I have done that for you."

The incredulity etched into Tyler's features deepened. "You honestly want me to marry a woman you met in the mountains of Maine on one of your fishing expeditions?"

"She's good wholesome stock and will produce the kind of grandchildren I want." Uriah stood and, placing his palms flat on the desk in the same manner as his son, leaned forward to bring his face to within inches of Tyler's. "If you want sole control of this company, you will do as I ask."

Tyler scowled. "And if I don't?"

"Then I will divide my voting shares between you and your brother and sister. You have shares of your own that would still leave you in control—" Uriah paused to give emphasis to his next words "—unless they decide to vote together against you."

"All either of them knows how to do is spend money!" Tyler growled. "They'd run this business into bankruptcy within a year!"

"If you don't marry and produce heirs, they or their offspring will eventually inherit control anyway," Uriah pointed out matter-of-factly, reseating himself.

Straightening, Tyler viewed his father narrowly. "Then I will find my own wife."

Uriah's expression hardened. "You will marry Kate Riley."

For a long moment the younger man regarded the older one in silence. Then, turning abruptly, he stormed out of the office. "Get me Harvey Stone!" he commanded his secretary as he crossed the hall to his own office and slammed the door behind him.

"Yes, sir," Blanche Olson replied to the closed door. She had seen Tyler Langston angry before, but never like this. Dialing Harvey's number, she said, "Harvey, this is Blanche. My boss wants to see you and he looks like he could breathe fire."

Harvey Stone was in Tyler's office in less than four minutes. "Blanche said you wanted to see me," he addressed the back of the man standing and looking out of the twelfth-story window at the landscaped grounds of the Langston industrial complex.

Turning from the window, Tyler faced his chief of security grimly. "I have a private matter I want you to take care of personally. It's family business. I'll pay you for your time, and I want only the original of your report—in your handwriting—and no copies. Once you've finished, I will keep the report and you will forget you ever did this service for me."

"Yes, sir," Harvey said, nodding. "May I assume that a woman is involved?"

The brown eyes that watched Harvey Stone darkened dangerously, making the man wish that he had kept this remark to himself. Walking over to his desk, Tyler scribbled a name and address on a sheet of paper and handed it to the security man. "I want to know everything you can find out about this person and I want the information by tomorrow afternoon."

IT WAS LATE the next evening when Tyler knocked on the door of his father's study in Uriah's private wing of the large family estate.

"Have you decided to obey my wishes," the elder Langston asked, watching his son cross the room, "or are you prepared, once I'm dead and buried, to spend the rest of your days battling your brother and sister over every decision you want to make regarding Langston Industries?"

Coming to a halt in the middle of the room, Tyler stood rigidly, staring at his father, who was seated in one of the leather wing chairs in front of the enormous old stone fireplace. "Kate Riley is an auto mechanic working a two-pump garage in a one-horse town. She has a high school education and no other training. Socially she would be completely out of place here. Surely you cannot be so insensitive as to want to embarrass both her and me.''

"I see you've done a little checking." Uriah smiled. Then the smile became a frown. "But your picture is only a surface view. The woman is more widely read than most of my friends and has developed a certain air of culture."

Tyler's eyes darkened. "You were under duress when you met her. Your car had broken down and you were stuck in Piperville for four days waiting for parts to arrive. By the end of that time, anyone who could speak in complete sentences would have seemed cultured."

"I *chose* to be stuck in Piperville for four days *after* I met Mrs. Riley." Uriah regarded his son levelly. "You know perfectly well I could have had those parts delivered within a day if I'd wished it."

"And that's another thing," Tyler went on, refusing to give up his fight. "*Mrs.* Riley was married at sixteen to a man twice her age."

"And widowed when she was twenty-two," his father finished. "I would venture to say that marriage is still an honorable institution. Don't try to tell me that those females you have spent time with didn't have their first rolls in the hay at an early age."

Tyler sucked in an angry breath. "If you are so smitten with this woman, why don't you marry her yourself!"

Uriah shook his head sadly. "I'm too old. Kate needs someone with youth and energy to handle her."

"Then give her to Ross!"

"Your brother wouldn't be able to control her for a minute. No—" Uriah looked his son hard in the face "—she's a perfect match for you."

Massaging the back of his neck, Tyler paced across the room. He had never seen his father so adamant. Finally stopping in front of Uriah's chair, he said curtly, "Six months!"

"What?" Uriah frowned.

"I will agree to a six-month trial marriage," Tyler conceded through clenched teeth.

Uriah rejected the concession. "Six months is not a trial—it's a childish fling," he said. "If you must have a limit, then we'll make it five years."

"One year," Tyler growled.

"Four."

Tyler ground his teeth. "We'll use Claire's first marriage as a precedent. I will agree to two years, and that is my limit!"

"Using your sister to set any precedent makes my skin crawl." Uriah frowned. "However, I will agree."

KATE FRANKLIN RILEY leaned under the hood of Sam Krammer's old Dodge and pulled out the worn spark plugs. It had been one of those days when there weren't enough minutes in an hour. Tomorrow was the beginning of a long Fourth of July weekend for a lot of people, and she had had three times as many gas customers as usual, as well as people wanting car tune-ups before starting out on long trips. Sam Krammer had come in during the middle of the afternoon, explaining that he had promised his wife that he would take her to visit her sister, but he was having so much trouble with his car he was worried about it breaking down halfway there. Considering all of the other jobs she had piled in front of her, Kate had been tempted to refuse to work on it, but Sam was a long-time customer and friend. And she needed the money.

With three other people besides herself to support, she always needed the money, she thought tiredly, glancing at the clock. Eight-thirty, and she still had to change the oil and lube the car. Normally she would have closed at eight and finished in the morning, but she had promised Sam his car tonight.

The ringing of the bell, indicating that someone had pulled up at the gas pumps, brought an under-the-breath curse. She had been so intent on getting Sam's car finished that she had forgotten to lock the pumps and turn off the outside lights at eight.

"Oh, well, what's one more interruption," she muttered acidly as she wiped the excess grease from her hands onto her coveralls and walked outside.

Because it was still early summer, the days were long, and the sun was slowly setting over the mountains to the west. But Kate didn't notice the colorful sky as her eyes fell on her customer. Climbing out of the silver-gray Porsche parked beside her pumps, he looked as out of place in this small Maine town as his car, and she guessed that the casual shirt, slacks and shoes he wore cost more than her entire wardrobe. The agitation on his face gave sharp definition to his angular features, heightening the squareness of his jaw. He was probably lost, she thought as she approached, pulling a red rag from her back pocket to finish wiping the grease from her hands.

His scowl deepened as she reached him. "You don't carry the highest grade."

She had heard this same complaint before from tourists, but the annoyance in this man's voice, mingled with her own fatigue, brought a flash of anger to her eyes. "I carry what my usual customers buy. I doubt if one tankful of the regular unleaded will ruin your car."

Tyler Langston studied the woman in front of him, from her short-cropped black hair to the curious gray-black eyes that regarded him with evident irritation, and down the five-foot, five-inch frame clothed in ill-fitting coveralls that hid her curves—if indeed there were any. Damn his father, he cursed silently, again wondering if Uriah was serious about him marrying this female. Aloud he said, "I suppose you're right. Fill it up."

She was tempted to tell him that the pumps were locked for the night. There was an arrogance in the way he was looking at her, as if she were an insect he'd like to crush. But business was money and, unscrewing the cap of the gas tank, she inserted the nozzle.

Leaning against the side of the car, Tyler shifted his attention from the woman to the garage. Old and in need of repair, it was still neat in appearance. "Where's Toby?" he asked, already knowing the answer but wondering what she would say.

"What?" Frowning, Kate glanced toward him.

"The sign says Toby's Garage." Tyler indicated the large letters over the entrance with a nod of his head. "I'm surprised he would leave a woman in charge."

"Toby was my husband. He left this place to me when he died, and I chose to keep the name the same," Kate replied cuttingly, "because there are a lot of sexist tourists passing through who wouldn't consider allowing a woman to touch their cars. Besides, the townspeople would have kept on calling it Toby's Garage no matter what I renamed it." Pulling out the nozzle, she screwed the cap back on the gas tank. "That'll be twenty dollars."

Pulling out a leather wallet, the man extracted a twenty-dollar bill and handed it to her.

Kate was doubly conscious of the grime beneath her fingernails as she accepted it, and with only a lowly muttered thank-you, she stalked into the garage and put the money in the till.

As the man drove away, she found herself glancing at her image in the mirror beside the Coke machine. There were grease smears on her face and neck, and her hair, which had begun the day in soft waves, was now a tangled mass of uncoordinated curls. Her clothes reeked of oil and gasoline and her hands looked as if they hadn't been washed in years. Then her back stiffened. No one had the right to look down on her as if she were less than human. She ran a legitimate business that kept her and her mother and brother and sister clothed, fed and with a roof over their heads. Admittedly her mother did rent a room to tourists looking for a quiet, out-of-the-way place to stay during the summer season, but that brought in only a small amount. It was Kate who carried the major burden of support.

Forcefully shaking off the sudden depressing effect the offensive customer had on her, she locked the pumps, turned off the outside lights and returned to Sam's car.

But later, when she washed up before going home, she took care to clean her hands and nails as thoroughly as possible.

She was exhausted as she drove home, and turning onto the street on which the old two-story, wood-framed house where she lived with her mother and brother and sister stood, she wondered if she was having an exhaustion-produced nightmare. On the street in front of the house sat the silver-gray Porsche.

Her mother met her at the door. A fragile-looking woman, as tall as her daughter but so thin she looked as if lifting a feather might be a strain, with chestnut hair streaked with gray, Harriet had blue eyes that almost continually held an edge of panic. "You smell like gasoline," she said reprovingly.

"That's probably because I make our living by operating a garage," Kate tossed back irritably.

"Well, go shower." A sparkle entered Harriet Franklin's eyes. "I have a guest I want you to meet."

"I'm not in the mood. As soon as I've showered, I'm going to bed." Kate headed for the stairs. She had no desire to face the haughty stranger again tonight.

"But it's Tyler Langston, Uriah Langston's son," her mother persisted, her face bright with excitement. "He said that his father was so impressed with his stay here with us that he decided to spend a few days here himself."

Uriah Langston had left both Kate and her mother large tips for fixing his car and boarding him during his stay in their town, and Kate could almost see the dollar signs in her mother's eyes. But the thought of spending any time under the same roof with the man who drove the silver-gray Porsche made Kate's blood run cold. "You spend a few days with him. I have more important things to do with my time." Feeling a sudden prickling sensation, her gaze traveled past her mother to the entrance to the living room to discover the object of their conversation watching them. Again she had the distinct impression that he considered her something less than human. Tilting her chin defiantly, she headed up the stairs.

A knock sounded on the bathroom door as she stripped and started to climb into the tub.

"Mom sent me up to get your clothes before they stink up the bathroom," Robin, the female half of the nine-year-old set of twins who were her brother and sister, said through the door.

Glad to get rid of the smell of gasoline, Kate gratefully shoved the clothing out the door to the blond-haired blue-eyed child, then proceeded to take a shower. She would have enjoyed a more leisurely bath, but there was only one bathroom in the house and it had to be shared. As she closed her eyes to rinse the shampoo from her hair, the image of their boarder came strongly into her mind, and she was glad she had taken the time to clean her hands and nails with extra care. Then, angry with herself for even caring what he thought of her, she turned off the water and toweled herself dry with excessive vigor. Pulling on a short terry cloth robe, she was about to leave the bathroom when her eyes fell on an expensive, tooled-leather shaving kit. For a long moment she stood staring at it, then again started to leave. But before her hand reached the doorknob, she stopped again and turned back toward the shaving kit. It was open, and picking it up, she noticed a small silver plaque discreetly attached to the inside. The inscription read: "Feel free to leave your shaving kit in my bathroom anytime. Love, Linda."

With a grimace of distaste, Kate zipped it shut and carried it out of the bathroom. Knocking on the door of the room directly across from her own, she waited for an answer. There was none. Her mother was obviously still plying their guest with apple pie and flattery. He could do without the flattery, she mused sarcastically, the inscription inside the leather kit still clear in her mind.

Indecisively she frowned at the shaving kit in her hand, and then, with a mental shrug, opened the door and entered. Crossing to the bed, she placed the kit on the night table.

Suddenly footsteps sounded in the hall, and she turned back toward the door just as Tyler Langston's muscular bulk blocked the exit. "Looking for me?" he asked dryly.

"I was returning your shaving kit," she said tightly, the brown eyes traveling over her robe-clad body making her feel uneasy and defensive. "The bathroom is community property and the twins feel free to inspect anything they find left in there. Your room, however, is private and out of bounds for them."

He continued to regard her darkly. Without the grease smears, the woman's unusually large gray eyes dominated a face that Tyler judged more cute than pretty. The nose was small and the lips were full. It was just the sort of face that would appeal to the protective instincts of an older man like his father, he mused cynically. Aloud he said, "Obviously you don't have the same respect for my privacy."

There was an edge to his voice that suggested he thought she might have been snooping through his things. Her back stiffened with indignation. "I knocked. There was no answer, so I came inside and put your shaving kit on the table. Now, if you will excuse me, I'll be on my way.''

But he didn't move, continuing instead to block the doorway. ''Do you make a habit of wandering into the room of a male guest wearing nothing more than a bathrobe?''

The way he spoke made her sound cheap, and her eyes flashed fire. ''I was merely trying to be helpful. In your case, however, I will stifle the impulse in the future. Now, get out of my way!''

Still he did not move. ''My father was quite taken with you.''

The implication in his voice was blatant, and her cheeks burned scarlet. ''Your father was a gentleman at all times, and if you don't get out of my way, I'm going to start screaming.''

The cynical smile with which he'd been regarding her deepened as he moved a little to one side.

She was forced to brush against him to make good her escape, and the unwelcome contact produced a strong sense of unease she could not shake as she entered her own room and dried her hair.

Her stomach began to growl, and pulling on a fresh pair of jeans and a T-shirt, she went downstairs and into the kitchen.

''I was just on my way to bed.'' Harriet's hand came up to cover a yawn as she turned away from the sink to see her daughter enter. ''But if you're hungry, I'll fix you something.''

"I can forage for myself," Kate said, refusing the halfhearted offer. "But I want Mr. Langston out of this house tomorrow."

Her mother frowned. "I realize you provide the largest share of our money, but I do contribute by taking in boarders, and Mr. Langston has already paid for a week in advance—and the twins need new clothes for school."

"I just don't trust the man," Kate said, scowling.

"He seemed like such a gentleman to me," Harriet murmured, alarm beginning to show on her face.

Watching her mother's expression and knowing that Harriet was jumping to some wild conclusions, Kate said, "I don't mean to imply that he might murder all of us during the night. I just meant he makes me uncomfortable."

"Oh." Her mother breathed a sigh of relief. "He does have a strong, domineering air about him and that has always made you a bit nervous about a man.... Speaking of men, Joe Nieley came by today. He said that you turned down his invitation to the Fourth of July Picnic."

"I'm not certain if I even want to go," Kate muttered, wishing there was a way to escape what was coming next and knowing there wasn't.

"I admit that Joe is quite a bit older than you, but so was Toby, and Joe's quite a bit wealthier. He owns the bank and a lot of land in these parts, not to mention an interest in a resort in New Hampshire. You could do a lot worse. You're twenty-seven years old

now and you aren't going to get many more chances."
Her mother's voice took on a coaxing tone. "I don't
understand why you won't marry him. You wouldn't
have to work in that smelly garage any longer, and I
wouldn't have to take in boarders who make you feel
uneasy. Joe told me today that if you marry him, he
would consider it his family duty to support all of us."

"We're doing just fine as we are," Kate said tersely,
passing her mother and opening the refrigerator.

"You married Toby Riley to better your situation." Harriet's voice took on a certain sharpness. "I
don't see why you can't marry Joe to better all of our
lives."

"Because..." Kate began, swinging around to face
her mother, her eyes darkening. The rest of what she
was going to say died in her throat as she saw Tyler
Langston standing in the doorway.

Following her daughter's line of vision, Harriet
Franklin turned. Seeing her boarder, she smiled politely. "Is there something I can do for you?"

Returning her smile with one that didn't quite reach
his eyes, he said, "I wanted to apologize to your
daughter. I'm afraid I may have said a few things she
took the wrong way."

With an exasperated grimace at Kate, Harriet returned her attention to Tyler. "She does have a habit
of taking things the wrong way. Knowing her sharp
tongue, she should probably be the one apologizing to
you. Now if you will excuse me, I think I'll retire."

Turning back to the refrigerator as her mother left the room, Kate uncovered a plate of fried chicken and took out a thigh. Then she poured herself a glass of milk and carried her late evening snack to the table.

In spite of a determined attempt to ignore the continued male presence in the room, she could feel Tyler's eyes following her.

The T-shirt revealed full breasts, and the jeans showed a small waist with pleasingly rounded hips. Tyler grudgingly admitted that he had always been partial to women with hourglass figures. However, the fact that this woman was being forced on him made her less than desirable. "I do want to apologize," he said stiffly, breaking the silence in the room as he seated himself across the table from her.

Glancing up, she met his shuttered gaze. "Your apology is accepted. Now will you please leave me alone."

Ignoring her request, he continued to study her coolly. "Even in this enlightened age there are relatively few female mechanics. How did you happen to choose that profession?"

"It was my husband's trade and he taught it to me," she answered tightly. Then again meeting his gaze, she frowned. "Why did you ask me about Toby? You obviously knew who I was when you stopped for gas."

"The truth is that my father told me very little about your personal life," he replied nonchalantly. He wasn't lying. It had been Harvey Stone who had supplied him with what details he had, and those were sketchy. Harvey hadn't had much time to do his research, and the Piperville townsfolk were not willing to discuss one of their own with a stranger. In carefully schooled conversational tones he asked, "How long have you had the responsibility for your mother and brother and sister on your shoulders?"

As she stared into the glass of milk, the lines of tiredness on Kate's face deepened. "My father died when I was nineteen. Toby and I helped my mother financially, and when Toby died, I sold our home and moved back in here. It was cheaper than supporting two households."

"Why don't you marry Joe Nieley like your mother wants you to?"

Shocked by his forwardness, her eyes narrowed as she again met his steady gaze. "Because I don't want to. I can take care of my family just fine on my own."

"Your mother seems to feel otherwise," he pointed out dryly.

Her jaw tightened. "My mother is a very nervous, very anxious person who grew up believing that a woman has to have a man to look after her no matter what the price."

A hint of cynicism entered Tyler's eyes. "You must have agreed with her at one time. You did marry when you were sixteen."

Kate's hands closed around the glass of milk. "I had my reasons, but they're none of your business." Rising abruptly from the table, she drank the milk as she walked to the sink. She placed the glass on the counter and moved toward the door. Pausing with her hand on the knob, she turned once more toward the unwelcome boarder. "If you're ready to go upstairs, I'll follow and turn off the lights. If not, you can turn them off yourself. I've had a long day and I'm beat."

"It's been a long day for me, too," Tyler said, rising from his chair and moving past her out the door.

As she followed him up the stairs, Kate thought about how confidently she had declared she could take care of her family. But the reality of the situation was that at this moment things were not going well. Business had been slow during the past winter, and both her mother and the twins had been ill, running up large medical bills.

But the thought of marrying Joe Nieley made her blood run cold. She couldn't do that to herself—nor to Toby. Climbing into bed a little while later, she vowed she would find another way to keep her family solvent.

# CHAPTER TWO

As USUAL, at a little before six the next morning, Kate was dressed for work and fixing herself some breakfast when John, the other twin, entered the kitchen. He was dressed in old blue jeans and a worn T-shirt, and his thick chestnut hair was brushed smooth. He regarded his sister from behind solemn brown eyes. "I'm coming to the garage with you today. I can pump the gas."

"All right," Kate agreed, lovingly ruffling his hair. Only nine and a little small for his age at that, he couldn't do much around the garage, but he tried and she enjoyed his company. "I'll throw a couple more eggs into the skillet. You'll need the energy. Tomorrow is the Fourth, so we'll probably be pumping a lot of gas today."

Smiling brightly, the boy opened the bag of bread. "I'll make the toast."

"And I'll make my own eggs when you're finished," Tyler Langston said from the doorway.

Startled by his early-morning appearance, Kate glanced toward their boarder and frowned. "You're up early."

Crossing the room, he leaned against the wall, his expression shuttered as he watched her turn the eggs. "I'm used to starting my day early."

"It's no trouble to cook two more eggs," she said stiffly, finding his proximity unnerving. "How do you want them?"

"Over easy," he answered, following her with his eyes as she crossed to the refrigerator, took out two more eggs and returned to the stove.

"You want toast, too?" John offered.

"Sure," Tyler replied, his gaze never leaving Kate. Again she had the impression he was studying her as if she were something less than human. "As long as you've joined the working class for breakfast, you can help by getting out the glasses and pouring the orange juice," she said tightly.

"Yes, ma'am." A dry smile tilted the corners of Tyler's mouth as he straightened away from the wall.

"The glasses are in there." John indicated a cabinet above his head.

By the time the last batch of eggs was removed from the skillet, Tyler had poured the orange juice and John was setting a plate of toast on the table.

Looking at the man in his tailor-made clothes, while she herself was in her coveralls and John was in his worn jeans and T-shirt, Kate couldn't help thinking they were a very unlikely trio.

John, on the other hand, seemed perfectly comfortable in the man's company. "I'm going to help

Kate at the garage today," he announced proudly between bites of egg and toast.

"I used to go into work with my father when I was your age," Tyler said approvingly.

"My dad's dead." John took a swallow of orange juice, then placing his glass aside, he looked at the man sitting across from him and added solemnly, "When he found out that he was going to be the father of twins, he went out to celebrate and got his neck broke in a fight at the tavern."

Kate felt a flush creeping from her neck onto her face. A few years before, John had begun asking questions about how his father had died. Their neighbor, who was one of the town's busiest busybodies, had been happy to fill him in on the sordid details of his father's drinking and brawling. To ease the picture, Harriet had added the celebration aspect, and the matter-of-fact statement he'd made to Tyler was the version John had developed to satisfy himself.

In Tyler Langston's estimation, Kate guessed, her family had just sunk a notch lower, and considering the way he kept looking at her as if he questioned her membership in the human race, she surmised that that put them somewhere below sea level. Furious with herself that she even cared what the man thought, she lifted her head to meet his gaze, pride glittering in her eyes.

His expression was shuttered. "I was wondering," he said, breaking the sudden uncomfortable silence, "if I could use the phone in your study. I have a few business calls to make. I will, of course, use my credit card.''

''We don't have a study,'' John said, frowning up at the man questioningly.

''He means my office,'' Kate explained, referring to the room off the living room where she kept her business files and housed her bills and records in a large, ancient rolltop desk. Shifting her attention to Tyler, she said, ''Yes, you may use the phone, but don't move anything on the desk. It may look like clutter, but I know where everything is.''

''Not anymore, you don't,'' John said knowingly. ''After Mr. Langston arrived yesterday, Mom had one of her tidying fits and shoved everything into the top lefthand drawer.''

Suppressing a groan, Kate took a final drink of her coffee. After carrying her plate to the sink, she scribbled a note to her mother informing her that John was coming to the garage. Sticking the note to the refrigerator with a magnet decorated with a bit of plastic fruit, she glanced toward her brother. ''Are you about ready to leave?''

The boy was out of his chair in a flash. Carrying his plate to the sink, he placed it on top of hers, then hurried out the back door.

Pausing in the doorway, Kate turned back toward Tyler. ''My mother will be up around seven,'' she informed him coolly, then followed her brother outside, glad to be away from the man's scrutiny. The way he continued to study her as if she were some kind of peculiar insect grated on her nerves.

The morning went reasonably well. John washed the front windshields of the cars and pumped the gas so that Kate only had to stop working in the garage to handle the cash register.

She had just slammed down the hood of the truck she'd been working on and was wiping the grease from her hands when a familiar voice sounded from the entrance.

"You could get arrested for using child labor," Joe Nieley admonished her. It was as close to a joke as he ever came but it still somehow fell short of humor.

Turning toward the entrance, Kate watched him make his way toward her, being careful not to step in any grease spots with his Italian leather shoes or get his three-piece suit dirtied by the tools hanging on the walls. He was forty-four, and his once-lean frame was beginning to take on a slightly rounded appearance, which enhanced his air of prosperity. By most standards he was a handsome man, distinguished looking, with strands of white beginning to work their way firmly through his once coal-black hair.

"John insisted on helping," she said, attempting to smile but failing. She didn't like Joe and she didn't trust him.

"If you'd give up this crusade to prove you can take care of yourself and your family on your own and marry me, you wouldn't have to spend your days working in this filthy garage." Disgust etched itself into his features as he looked around. "Toby Riley certainly fell short of providing for his widow."

"He did the best he could," Kate snapped. Then, because Joe was a powerful man, she mentally counted to ten and, leaning against the truck, forced a politeness into her voice. "I do appreciate your offer, but I'm not interested in remarrying."

Joe's thin veneer of civility fell away, exposing the anger beneath. Forgetting the dirt and grease, he closed the distance between himself and Kate in one long stride and, capturing her by the upper arms, glared down into her face. "Toby Riley might have been a great lover, but his memory won't keep your family fed or a roof over their heads."

"Let go of me," she hissed through clenched teeth.

The fingers holding her arms dug deeper. "You are the only thing in this world that Toby Riley ever really cared about, and one way or another I'm going to have you."

Hatred mingled with the anger in the man's face, and Kate felt a cold rush of fear. She had always suspected that Joe's proposals had more to do with his hatred of Toby than with any love he felt for her, but hearing him admit it was a shock. "Let go of me," she repeated, this time attempting to twist free from his grasp.

"I think you should do as the lady asks," came a hard voice from the doorway. It was Tyler Langston's.

Joe glanced over his shoulder and his expression blackened further. Turning back to Kate, he said in low threatening tones that held no compromise, "I will win, Kate." Releasing her abruptly, he walked out of the garage as if he was in total control of the situation.

As she watched him leave, Kate drew a worried breath. Then she schooled her features into a mask of indifference and turned her attention to Tyler. "What are you doing here?"

"Your mother was going to bring you and John some lunch," he answered. "I was coming this way anyway, so I volunteered to save her the trip."

"You really made Mr. Nieley mad this time, Sis," John said, coming up behind Tyler, then slipping past him to approach Kate. "He nearly broke the window of his car when he slammed the door shut, and he drove away without waiting for his change."

John extended a ten-dollar bill toward her. Taking it from him, Kate went into the small windowed office area and punched a key on the cash register.

Tyler followed and set the basket he was carrying on the counter. Regarding her with a scowl, he said, "I suppose my father met Mr. Nieley when he was in town."

"Yeah," John responded when his sister remained silent. "He's always hanging around Kate."

"Go wash your hands so you can eat lunch," Kate ordered, interrupting any further comments John might have been thinking of making. Studying Tyler

Langston suspiciously, she waited until the boy was gone, then demanded icily, "Why are you here, Mr. Langston?"

"To bring you your lunch," he replied dryly.

"Don't be obtuse!" she said, glaring. "I want to know why you are in this town staying with me and my family."

His level gaze revealed nothing of what was going on in his mind. "My father said your mother had a pleasant room to rent and was a good cook, and I felt that I needed a vacation in a quiet little town with a pleasant, relaxed atmosphere." Then before she could express her doubts about the validity of this statement, he added, "Enjoy your lunch," and left.

As she watched him drive away, Kate's frown deepened. Tyler Langston was definitely out of place in this one-horse town. He belonged in an expensive country club with an equally expensive blonde hanging on his arm. She recalled the remarks he had made about his father and remembered how paternal Uriah Langston's behavior had been toward her. It dawned on her then that the elder Langston might be considering doing something to ease her situation. A cynical smile played across her face. If the father had a plan, it was obviously one the son disapproved of. Suddenly the reason for the way Tyler had been watching her became clear. He was looking for something to use to dissuade his father from whatever action Uriah might be considering.

Well, he didn't have to worry, she thought acidly. She had no intention of taking advantage of Uriah Langston's chivalrous nature.

"JOHN TELLS ME you quarreled with Joe today," Harriet said in disapproval as she joined her daughter on the porch that evening.

Kate had taken her brother home at five but had returned to the garage and kept it open until eight. Then she had come home, showered and made herself a sandwich, which she carried outside to eat, curled up on the porch swing and seeking the quiet solitude of the night. "I didn't quarrel with him. I merely refused his offer of marriage," she replied, adding in an uncompromising voice, "and I don't want to talk about it. I've had a rough day, and all I want to do is to eat in peace."

Harriet's disapproving look deepened. "You're becoming very difficult to live with. I realize you have a great load on your shoulders, but Joe has always been very kind to me and he loves you."

"He doesn't love me," Kate stated flatly.

"I don't know how you can say that," her mother admonished. "He has courted you for the past five years, ever since Toby's death. He's been very patient and understanding, too."

"Mom, please." Kate's voice held a strong note of exasperation. "I don't want to talk about Joe Nieley. I don't want to talk about anything. I just want to be alone for a while."

Breathing a frustrated sigh, Harriet shook her head. "I honestly don't understand you. You have a wealthy, respectable man who wants to marry you, and yet you insist on working yourself to a frazzle at that garage. Running a garage is a man's job!"

Kate rewarded her mother with a cold stare, and with a discouraged shake of her head, Harriet went back inside.

Alone again, Kate stared unseeing at the crescent moon surrounded by thousands of stars. Her mother was right about one thing. Joe Nieley had been patient. But the look on his face and the actual mention of Toby's name earlier that day told her that his patience had come to an end. Leaning her head back, she closed her eyes. She was painting troubles before they came. What could Joe do?

"Mind if I join you?" Tyler Langston's voice broke the peaceful stillness.

"Yes," she answered coldly, opening her eyes to discover him seating himself on the swing in spite of her blunt rejection of his company.

"Your mother seems to think that marrying Joe Nieley is the perfect solution to all of your problems."

Her jaw tightened as she concentrated on a brightly twinkling star. "My mother doesn't have all of the facts."

"Such as how much he disliked your former husband?"

Kate's gaze swung to the man, her eyes darkening. "Do you always eavesdrop on other people's conversations?"

The hint of a cynical smile curled his lips. "It looked more like the beginning of a brawl to me."

With a stay-out-of-my-business glare, Kate rose from the swing and started toward the door.

But before she could make good her escape, Tyler blocked her way. Catching her by the arm, he pulled her into a darkened corner of the porch and pinned her against the house with his body.

Startled, she raised her hands and pressed them against the solid wall of his chest. She could feel the steady beat of his heart beneath her palms, and her throat felt suddenly dry. Her acute awareness of him as a man shocked and frightened her.

"Your mother tells me you haven't dated anyone since your husband's death," Tyler said in low tones. "Are you really that immune to men?"

As he spoke, his hands moved leisurely along her sides, pausing momentarily to allow his thumbs to test the curve of her breasts, then continuing downward to her hips.

She drew a hard sharp breath as the heat of his touch sparked a fire in her of startling intensity.

"Stop that or I'll scream," she threatened in a terse whisper.

"And bring the entire neighborhood running," he chided, calling her bluff.

She opened her mouth to protest again, but before any sound could come out, his lips found hers and accepted their parted position as an invitation to deepen the kiss.

Her hands, splayed against his chest, offered little resistance. The hard musculature of his thighs pressed against her sent the blood surging hot and wild through her veins.

His mouth left hers to travel to the hollow of her throat. He kissed the throbbing pulse, then raised his head to look into her eyes, heavy-lidded now with desire.

"No, you are not immune," he said softly.

Frightened and angered by the traitorous reaction of her body, Kate violently twisted free and fled into the house.

In her room, she discovered she was shaking. She didn't even like Tyler Langston, but he had brought her body to life as if it had been merely waiting for his touch.

IT WAS THE FOURTH OF JULY. The garage was closed and Kate gave herself the luxury of sleeping late.

But the Fourth of July Picnic was the biggest social event of the year in Piperville, and Kate's self-awarded luxury lasted only until eight o'clock when the twins burst into her room demanding she get up.

"Mom says that if Mr. Langston doesn't get up soon, you'll have to take her pies over to the picnic grounds," Robin said excitedly. "She doesn't want to miss entering them in the pie-judging contest. She's been working on this recipe for gooseberry-and-rhubarb pie all year and she's sure she'll win first place." Robin managed to get it all out in one breath, parroting what Harriet had said when she sent the children upstairs to wake their sister.

Groaning, Kate pulled the pillow over her head. Immediately Robin and John grabbed hold and tried to pull it off. This was a game the three had played since Kate had first moved in with them when the twins were barely four years old.

"You get her feet," Robin ordered her brother between giggles, and before Kate could move to protect herself, John had uncovered her feet and was tickling them.

"No fair!" she cried, tossing the pillow aside as she squirmed into a sitting position and captured both youngsters in her arms. Laughing, she kissed each one on the forehead. "All right, all right. You win. I'll get up as soon as you leave and give me some privacy to pull myself together," she bargained.

"As long as you promise not to go back to sleep," Robin stipulated.

"Promise." Kate grimaced woefully. Then feeling a sudden uneasiness, she glanced toward the door to discover that the twins had left it open and that Tyler Langston was leaning against the doorjamb of his room across the hall, watching their antics. "And close the door on your way out," she added, pulling the covers up in front of her in an unconscious defensive gesture.

She felt his eyes on her until the door closed between them, and as she climbed out of bed, she admitted to herself that he frightened her.

Brushing her hair, she heard the twins attempting to persuade Tyler to join them at the picnic. To her dismay, he agreed. She hadn't wanted to go to the picnic in the first place. Now she doubly didn't want to go.

A little while later, looking through the limited assortment of clothes in her closet, she was tempted to dress for comfort in jeans and a blouse, but finally she instead pulled out a pale pink eyelet sundress. The jeans would have brought the comment, "You're twenty-seven and you should dress appropriately for social occasions," from her mother, and every cell in her body rebelled against that statement being made in front of Tyler Langston. Her mother had a way of saying it that made Kate sound as if she was years past her prime.

Frowning, she looked at herself closely in the mirror. Admittedly she wasn't a teenager any longer. But one day when the twins were grown, she was going to leave this town and build a life for herself. Maybe she would even be lucky enough to find a man who would love her and she him.

But she wasn't going to settle for a Joe Nieley. She had made her compromises, and while she did not regret them, she would make no more.

Pulling on the dress, she slipped into a pair of low-heeled sandals, made a final quick examination of herself in the mirror, applied an extra touch of lipstick, then went downstairs.

Tyler had finished his breakfast and was sitting at the table, drinking a second cup of coffee and listening to the twins describe in detail the events of the day.

"There are races in the afternoon, and they have trophies for the winners," John was explaining enthusiastically. "Robin and I have been practicing the three-legged sack race ever since school was out, and if she doesn't trip, we're gonna win!"

Rewarding her brother with a scowl, Robin picked up the narrative. "And for the picnic all of the unmarried women will have lunch baskets on a long table and Mr. Jacobs will auction them off to the unmarried men. Mr. Nieley would be doing the auctioning because he's the mayor, but he's divorced so that makes him one of the bachelors." Robin grimaced. "He'll probably bid on Kate's basket."

"I'm not taking a basket," Kate stated as she opened the refrigerator and took out the orange juice.

"Yes, you are," Robin corrected. "Mom has already packed it."

"Then she can eat with whomever buys it," Kate returned curtly.

"Katherine, you will mind your manners," Harriet admonished sharply.

Pausing in the act of pouring herself a glass of juice, Kate turned toward her mother. "I told you I had no intention of participating in the basket auction when you told me that the committee had decided to introduce this little innovation this year, and I meant it.''

"It's a great lunch," John said in an attempt to soften the situation. Kate glared at her mother while Harriet remained steadfast in her determination that her daughter take a lunch.

"You can tell which one is Kate's by the big green bow on the handle," Robin told Tyler, her tone strongly suggesting that he should bid on the basket. "And if you bought it, you'd get to share it with Kate."

Harriet frowned at her younger daughter. "Mr. Tyler is our guest and will be sharing *our* basket," she said.

Embarrassed by the family dispute in front of Tyler and knowing that arguing would get her nowhere, Kate drank her orange juice in a terse silence. Then, after pouring herself a cup of coffee, she went out onto the porch and sat down on the porch swing. She knew she was going to have to face Joe Nieley again sometime. She just hadn't wanted it to be over a picnic lunch. Recalling how angry he had been with her the day before, the hope that he wouldn't bid on her lunch began to grow.

"Robin has been telling me that your mother made two small gooseberry-rhubarb pies for your basket, along with the fried chicken and deviled eggs," Tyler said, joining her on the porch, his tone indicating he was dubious about the pies.

Kate ignored him and took a sip of her coffee, her attention concentrated on the bright yellow lilies blooming in the garden beside the porch.

Tyler leaned against one of the pillars supporting the roof and continued to study her, the hint of a cynical smile playing at the corners of his mouth. "I tried to help. I suggested it might be unfair for you to take a basket of food that your mother had prepared. It might give the unsuspecting male who bought it the impression you could cook."

Kate met his cynical grin with one of her own. "I'll bet she loved hearing that."

The brown eyes twinkled. "You notice I have joined you on the porch."

"And I thought you only came out here to annoy me," she tossed back acidly.

"Annoyance wasn't what I saw in your eyes last night," he countered in low, mellow tones.

Swallowing hard, she turned her attention back to the flowers. She wanted to think of something witty and cutting to say, but the sudden recollection of how his lips and hands had touched her made thinking close to impossible.

"You'll have to carry your basket." Harriet's voice broke the silence that had descended over the porch as she came through the doorway with a large basket on each arm. "I have to carry both my picnic basket and my basket of pies. John has your basket, but I know he'll drag it halfway to the park if you let him carry it."

"Let me help you." Tyler was immediately at Harriet's side, taking the baskets from her.

Grudgingly taking her basket from John, Kate noted that the cynicism that had been etched into Tyler's features had vanished and that he was now exuding pure charm.

"Kate is a perfectly good cook," Harriet said haughtily, as she and Tyler descended the steps and started down the sidewalk. "The only reason I packed her lunch was because she doesn't have time to cook these days."

"I'm certain she's a wonderful cook," he said, smiling down at her warmly, his tone apologetic. "How could she not be with you for a teacher?"

Harriet blushed and rewarded him with a forgiving smile.

Watching from behind, Kate promised herself for the umpteenth time that she would never be as gullible as her mother when men were concerned.

The twins ran ahead of the adults, and Harriet, now that Tyler was back in her good graces, became completely absorbed in telling him again how much they had enjoyed his father's stay with them.

Walking more and more slowly, Kate fell several feet behind. The urge to continue fading from the group until she was far enough behind to slip away completely, return home, change into jeans and go find some secluded spot in which to spend the day was strong, and the distance between herself and the others increased.

It was Tyler who noticed she'd fallen behind. Glancing over his shoulder, he frowned and said something to her mother.

Harriet came to an impatient halt and looked back toward her daughter. "Kate, hurry up!"

"I didn't fade fast enough," Kate muttered to herself, picking up her pace as her mother began to tap her toe in annoyance.

As she caught up with them, Kate noticed a hint of amusement in Tyler's eyes. She realized he had guessed what had been on her mind and had purposely acted to prevent her escape. Casting him a hostile glance, she picked up her pace even more and caught up with the twins.

By the time they arrived, the park in the center of Piperville was already swarming with people.

Booths had been set up where, for a quarter, children and adults alike could test their skill at knocking down bowling pins with a softball, tossing rings around the tops of soda bottles, throwing darts at balloons or dunking one of the locals by hitting a bull's-eye at the end of a pole that held a chair above a tank of water.

One of the high school cheerleaders, in a scanty bikini, was in the chair at the moment, and the line of men and boys willing to spend a quarter to send her into the water was nearly as long as the park.

Lou Grady beamed at Harriet as she and the others paused momentarily to watch the action. "It's one of the best fund-raising schemes we've ever come up with," he said.

"I just hope she doesn't catch her death of cold," Harriet returned with a reproving frown, then continued toward the table where she was to hand in her pies for the judging.

Kate caught the approving wink Tyler shot at the man and experienced an unpleasant prickling sensation. Frowning at herself for letting his appreciation of the bikini-clad body bother her, she walked over to the auction table and unceremoniously plunked her basket into the middle of the collection already assembled there.

In spite of the fact that the names of the owners of the baskets were supposed to be secret until the bidders had made their purchases, several of the baskets had ribbons or brightly colored covers that told the bidders which baskets were whose.

A sudden smile lit Kate's face, and she began to untie the green ribbon.

"Kate," her mother's disapproving voice sounded behind her, "I told Joe that your basket would have a green ribbon on it and it will have a green ribbon on it!" Brushing her daughter aside, Harriet expertly retied the ribbon.

Tyler was smiling again, and Kate, grabbing each of the twins by the hand, tossed him a haughty glare and led the children toward the booths.

The morning, she noticed, seemed to drag on forever. After a couple of futile tries apiece by each twin to win a small stuffed animal, they were sent to play on the swings with some of their friends, and Kate found herself being dragged along with her mother and Tyler to the pie judging.

Single women who normally had no time for Kate came up to say hello to her, and as etiquette required, she introduced them to Tyler. Immediately their attention focused on him, while Kate mentally scoffed at their flirtatious antics. A man like Tyler Langston was not going to be interested in an unsophisticated small-town girl.

Increasingly annoyed by the constant stream of inane chatter and feeling a strong need to escape Tyler's company, she told her mother she was going to check on the twins. Leaving Harriet to introduce Tyler to whomever showed up next, she left the crowd around the pie-judging table and started back toward the swings.

Her ploy, however, was unsuccessful. Tyler shook loose his latest admirer by promising to dance with her at the dance that would follow the evening fireworks display and fell into step beside Kate. "I don't believe I've ever met so many unmarried females at one time."

Seeing the twins ahead playing happily on the swings, she came to a halt in the shade of a big old oak. Annoyance was stamped on her features as she looked up at her uninvited companion. "A new unattached male in town attracts them like moths to a flame."

As he leaned against the trunk of the tree, Tyler regarded her with dry amusement. "But you, of course, would never consider playing with fire." As he spoke, he gently trailed a finger down the line of her arm.

Goose bumps rose on her flesh. Jerking away, she fought back the rush of feeling that threatened to color her cheeks and said, "A person can get badly injured playing with fire."

The brown of his eyes darkened. "Are you speaking from experience?"

Her jaw tightened. "That, Mr. Langston, is none of your business."

"Kate!" Harriet's voice sounded from their left.

Turning to look, Kate saw her mother approaching with Joe Nieley. "How did the pie judging go?" she asked as they joined her and Tyler.

"I took second place," Harriet replied in disappointment. "The judges felt that Jane's cherry-apple pie was more patriotic."

Joe broke into the exchange. "I would have come looking for you sooner," he said, his gaze shifting from Kate to Tyler, then back to Kate. "But I was selling chances on the water dunk."

Suddenly more concerned about her daughter's future than her own failure to win the pie judging, Harriet forced a smile. "Joe, this is Tyler Langston. He's boarding with us for a few days. His father is Uriah Langston. I believe you met him when he was here a few weeks ago."

"Yes." Joe managed a smile that did not reach his eyes as he extended his hand to Tyler. Kate knew from the way his jaw twitched that he recognized Tyler as the man who had interrupted Joe and herself at the garage the day before.

Accepting the handshake, Tyler, too, smiled coldly. "Nice little town you have here."

Joe's smile faded as his mouth formed a hard, straight line. "I'm sure you must find it quite boring." Beneath the transparent veil of civility, the suggestion that Tyler should leave Piperville as soon as possible was blatant.

"As a matter of fact, I am enjoying it immensely," Tyler replied smoothly.

Glancing toward her mother, Kate saw the fear in her eyes and could almost read her mind. Harriet didn't want someone who was just passing through, as Tyler Langston was, interfering with her plans for her daughter to marry Joe Nieley.

"I think it must be almost time for the basket auction," Harriet said brightly, effectively putting a halt to the tense exchange. "You don't want to miss that, do you, Joe?"

"No, I don't," he agreed.

"Then you and Kate run along," Harriet directed. "Tyler is having lunch with the twins and me."

Joe offered Kate his arm. Momentarily she considered refusing it, but the look on her mother's face changed her mind, and slipping her arm through his, she allowed herself to be led toward the auction table.

"The way Langston has been hanging around you, I thought he might be considering bidding on your basket," Joe said coldly.

"Tyler Langston is not interested in me and I am not interested in him," she said flatly. The situation between her and Joe was touchy enough without adding any further cause for conflict. While she had no intention of marrying him, he was still one of the most influential men in town and life would be easier for her if she could avoid making him her enemy.

"That's good," he said.

Something in his voice caused her to glance up at his face, and the smile she saw there brought a strong wave of apprehension.

Her basket was the tenth to be auctioned.

"Twenty-five," Joe bid confidently.

Kate cringed. The bid was too high. People in the town would take it as a public declaration that he intended to marry her, and Joe never placed himself in a situation where he might come out looking like a loser. He wasn't going to accept her continued refusal easily.

"Thirty," a male voice from behind suddenly offered.

Swinging around, she saw Tyler. He was smiling with innocent nonchalance.

Joe's smile became a scowl. "Thirty-five."

"Forty," Tyler countered.

The auctioneer beamed. "Well, well, this certainly has turned into quite a fund-raiser," he said, while people who were not part of the auction suddenly stopped what they were doing to watch.

With an inward groan, Kate turned to glare angrily at Tyler. He was infuriating Joe, and that was going to make her life even more unpleasant.

"Fifty," Joe bid curtly.

"One hundred" came Tyler's easy response, his tone indicating he would go further if necessary.

"It appears your Mr. Langston enjoys playing games," Joe snarled at Kate.

"He's not *my* Mr. Langston," she replied sharply. "He just finds us and our ways amusing and likes to play games."

"Just keep in mind that I do not play," Joe warned threateningly, and with a contemptuous glance at Tyler to let the man know he refused to participate in a sideshow, he walked away.

"Seems your boarder has bought himself a lunch," the auctioneer said, smiling at Kate.

Glancing around, she saw people whispering and heard a few giggles. Mentally she cursed Tyler Langston. News of what had happened here was certain to spread through town like wildfire. Joe's pride would take a beating and he was only going to become more difficult than ever to reason with.

Tyler handed a one-hundred dollar bill to the cashier, who in return, gave him Kate's basket along with a bright curious smile.

"You really do enjoy making my life difficult," Kate muttered accusingly as he took her by the arm and led her away from the crowd.

"My life isn't going to be so easy, either." His smile was mischievous as he brought them to a halt in the shade of an old oak. "Your mother thinks I'm purchasing tickets on the water dunk. When she finds out what I've done, she's likely to have my bags on the porch when I return to the house."

For a moment, the appealing boyishness in his smile caused her heart to flutter, then she heard a twitter from one of the passing couples and a coldness swept over her. "This is not a joke."

Tyler's gaze lost its humor. "Are you telling me that in spite of all of your protests, you actually wanted to have lunch with that Nieley character?"

"No." Leaning against the trunk of the tree, she stared tiredly at the milling crowd that filled the park. "I just want to keep my life as smooth as possible. Joe is furious about this, and the ribbings he's going to get from folks are only going to make him madder."

Setting the basket on the ground, Tyler placed a hand on the trunk of the tree on either side of her. "And here I saw myself as your knight in shining armor."

As she looked up into the dark depths of his eyes, a strange chill shook her. He did make quite a dashing rescuer. Then reality returned. To him, this was a game and he hadn't rescued her; he had only made an unpleasant situation worse. "I have no use for a weekend warrior, Mr. Langston,'' she said stiffly. "Enjoy your lunch." Then slipping under one of his arms, she marched off. She wasn't certain where she was going. She just wanted to be alone. This time, choosing to let her escape, Tyler did not follow.

"Kate," Joe spoke her name grimly as he fell into step beside her a few minutes later. "I want to talk to you—alone."

She considered pleading a headache, but that would only be putting off the inevitable. Nodding her agreement, she allowed him to lead her across the street and around to the side of the bank. Opening the private entrance to his office, he stepped aside to allow her to enter ahead of him.

It was a large office for such a small bank. An oversize cherrywood desk flanked by two leather-upholstered wing chairs occupied one end of the room, and at the other end, a cherrywood table surrounded by chairs of the same wood sat on a round blue-and-beige Oriental rug.

"Please, make yourself comfortable," he said, waving a hand toward one of the chairs.

As she complied, he opened the cabinet built into the dark paneled walls of the room to expose a complete bar with a sink and small refrigerator. The array of glasses on the shelves, Kate knew, was fine crystal. She also knew that Joe Nieley hadn't created this room with its expensive furnishings just for show. It had been designed to intimidate. A prospective client or partner in one of Joe's many business ventures would enter this room and immediately feel that Joe was doing him a favor by seeing him, thus giving Joe the psychological advantage in any dealings.

Kate, however, was neither impressed nor intimidated. But she was apprehensive. There was a confidence in Joe's manner that worried her.

Opening the refrigerator, he took out a bottle of champagne and carried it, along with two glasses, to the table. As he began to unwrap the foil from the top of the bottle, he said, "I thought we would celebrate our engagement with a toast."

Kate's posture became rigid. "I have already told you I have no intention of remarrying."

"You will marry me," he informed her coldly. Pausing momentarily, he met her determined gaze with a frosty smile. "Or you will find yourself and your family in dire financial straits."

Her hand tightened on the arm of her chair as she fought to keep her voice level. "What do you mean by that?"

Setting the bottle aside, his eyes traveled over her leisurely as if savoring the moment. "I have been very patient with you, Kate. But my patience has come to an end. On my desk you will find a sheet of paper with a number on it. That is the amount of money your mother owes me."

Licking her suddenly dry lips, Kate rose and crossed the room to the desk. No amount of apprehension could have prepared her for the number written on the sheet of paper. Staring at it incredulously, she said in a low, harsh whisper, "I don't believe this."

"Haven't you ever wondered how your mother paid for your father's funeral? And her hospital bills after the twins were born?" he asked with cynical amusement. "You must remember that they were premature and required a great deal of special care."

"My father left insurance," she answered, realizing as she spoke that this was obviously a fabrication by her mother.

"Your father left nothing but a string of bar bills and gambling debts. Harriet was too embarrassed to go to you and Toby for help in paying them. Besides, that garage had never made enough for you to have accumulated the lump sum she needed." The smile on Joe's face deepened as he began removing the wire holding the cork in place on the champagne bottle. "So she came to me and I personally loaned her the necessary amount. Then, when the twins were born, we worked out another loan. Through the years, I have never pressed her to pay me back. She has given me small amounts once in a while, but I have also allowed her to borrow small amounts. Her payments have never kept up with her borrowing. Now those little loans tacked onto the original amount plus the interest I felt it was only fair to charge has added up to a tidy little sum, don't you think?"

"I'll pay you back every cent," Kate promised curtly.

"It would take you forever." Joe's smile vanished as his mouth formed a hard, straight line. "Besides, I am tired of playing games and I want to have a family before I'm too old to enjoy it. Unless you agree to marry me, I will call in the debt immediately. You will then have thirty days to come up with the money. I should also mention that part of the debt involves a second mortgage on the house in which you live, and that garage of yours is sorely outdated. You couldn't raise more than fifteen or twenty thousand and your mother owes me forty-seven plus change."

Kate's jaw tightened as she fought to keep her composure. He was right in his evaluation of her financial situation, but she refused to capitulate.

"Lloyd Martin came in the other day," he continued, the smile returning to his face. "His son is getting out of the army soon, and he was telling me that Lloyd, Jr. has been trained as a mechanic. It seems that the boy is thinking of opening a gas station a couple of miles out of town at the intersection with the main highway."

Kate could hear the nails being driven into her coffin. The locals came to her because she was one of them and her gas station was convenient. But Lloyd Martin, Jr. was also one of them, and his gas station would be just as convenient for many of her customers. In addition, he was a veteran and a man, both of which would weigh heavily in his favor.

"I need some time to think," she said stiffly.

"Take all afternoon," he offered, popping the cork from the bottle. "Just keep in mind that I want to announce our engagement at the dance tonight."

Pouring them each a glass of the sparkling wine, he carried her drink across the room and handed it to her. "To our future," he said.

As he clinked his glass against hers, she stood immobile. There had to be a way out of this, but at the moment, she couldn't think clearly enough to find it.

Regarding her with cool confidence, Joe smiled. "You should be happy to know that you are providing a secure future for your mother and the twins."

With the mention of her mother and the twins, the walls seemed to close in on Kate. She would rather live in abject poverty than marry Joe Nieley, but she had their lives to consider. "You can't really want to marry me," she said tightly.

"You're wrong," he assured her, his eyes traveling over her in a purely masculine inspection. "You are an attractive woman and I find the thought of taking you into my bed very appealing."

Disgust filled her. "You can't really want a woman that you've had to blackmail into your bed."

"You're so naive." Reaching across the table, he ran a finger along the line of her jaw. "If I cared about you, perhaps that would be the case. But to me, you are merely Toby Riley's widow, and because of that, the thought of taking you into my bed and having complete control over you is more exciting than I ever dreamed possible."

Until this moment, she had never realized how truly possessed Joe was by his hatred of her dead husband. She jerked away from his touch, and fear showed momentarily on her face.

As he watched her, his smile broadened. "Yes, I think I'm going to enjoy this very much." Then, glancing at his watch, he breathed a sigh of regret. "I'm afraid we have to end this enjoyable conversation. I'm due back at the park to judge the pie-eating contest in just a few minutes." Rising from his chair, he caught her chin in his hand and tilted her head to place a light kiss on her lips. "Until tonight." His intonation made it clear that he had more than just the announcement of their engagement in mind.

A little later Kate felt chilled, in spite of the hot July sun, as she stood with her mother and Tyler watching the children devour pieces of pie while holding their hands behind their backs.

"I spoke to Joe just before he began the judging," Harriet said, beaming at her daughter. With a side glance toward Tyler, she continued, "And I am now willing to forgive Mr. Langston for his behavior. Joe told me that the two of you had a very agreeable talk this afternoon."

Kate wanted to take her mother aside and demand to know how she could have placed her in this position, but Kate already knew the answer. Her mother was totally naive when men and money were concerned, and getting angry with her would not solve the problem. Instead, she forced herself to smile and nod.

She could feel Tyler's eyes on her but refused to look in his direction.

When the contest ended, Joe joined them, slipping a possessive arm around Kate's waist. Harriet's eyes danced while the twins looked at each other questioningly and Tyler watched cynically.

Kate's stomach churned and she had an almost uncontrollable urge to scream. If it wasn't for the twins, she'd pack up and leave Piperville by morning, never to return. Knowing that she had to get away from the picnic and have some time to herself to collect her thoughts, she said, "I don't feel very well. I think the sun is too much for me."

"You do look pale," Harriet said solicitously. "I'm always telling you to wear a hat, but you never listen to me."

Kate struggled to keep her voice civil. "I think I should go home and rest for a while."

"That would probably be a good idea," Harriet agreed. "I'll be bringing the twins home after the games to rest and have a little dinner before the fireworks begin tonight. You could nap until then and then you'll be fresh for the dance."

"If I didn't have to judge this next contest, I'd take you home," Joe said, smiling down on her.

The smile went no further than the corners of his mouth, and the look in his eyes turned Kate's blood to ice. "I can take myself home just fine," she assured him in carefully controlled polite tones.

"Perhaps I should walk you home just in case you begin to feel faint," Tyler offered.

Joe's hand tightened painfully on Kate's waist in warning.

"No," she said curtly, then added in milder tones, "The twins are anxious for you to see them compete in the three-legged sack race, and I wouldn't want them to be disappointed."

Joe relinquished his hold on her waist and said, "I'll come by and pick you up around eight for the fireworks."

"Fine," she muttered, then again forcing a smile, she waved goodbye and walked away from the group.

# CHAPTER THREE

ONCE OUT OF THEIR SIGHT, Kate quickened her pace. A few people said hello as she passed, but she only returned the greetings perfunctorily and didn't stop to talk. She needed to be alone. She had to think.

Back at the house, she paced the living room, then went into her small office and looked through her papers. Finding nothing there to give hope, she returned to the living room and resumed pacing. Tears of frustration began to trickle down her cheeks. There had to be a way out of this.

She climbed the stairs to her room, where she opened a drawer in her dresser and took out a photo album. Sitting on the bed, she opened it lovingly. Toby's face smiled up at her. It was a nice face, a kind face. Drawing a shaky breath, she recalled how sweet a man he had been.

The clock in the downstairs hall chimed the hour, and her hands tightened on the album. The others would be returning home soon, and she wasn't ready to face them.

Closing the album, she gently laid it back in the drawer, then quickly changed out of her dress and into a pair of old cut-off jeans and a T-shirt. She scribbled a note to her mother saying she had decided to go for a drive. Then after attaching the message to the refrigerator, she hurried out the front door.

"Going somewhere?" Tyler Langston's voice stopped her as she started down the porch stairs. She turned around to see him rising from the porch swing.

"I thought I'd go for a drive," she said, quickly resuming her move toward her car.

"Ever drive a Porsche?" he asked, as he caught up with her, then leaned against the door of her car so that she couldn't open it.

"No. Now, please get out of the way," she said, looking past him, worried that the others would return before she could make good her escape.

"Try mine." He grasped her hand and placed the keys to his car in it, then headed to the Porsche and climbed in the passenger side.

After a long moment, as she stood watching him, a contemplative expression crossed her face. Maybe there was a solution to one part of her problem, she thought. Reaching a decision, she approached the Porsche and climbed in behind the wheel.

As Tyler noticed her again looking worriedly down the street, he said, "I managed to make good my escape before the last race began. We still have a few minutes before the others start home."

She frowned at his ability to read her thoughts, then listened as he gave her brief instructions. She moved the seat forward to accommodate her shorter legs, then threw the car into gear.

Leaving town by a back road, she drove toward the ocean. The road twisted through rugged pine-forested terrain carved by glaciers thousands of years earlier.

The car sped, hugging the road securely, and her foot pressed harder and harder on the gas. The miles flew past as she lost herself in the fantasy of escape.

"Do I assume you know this road well?" Tyler asked curtly, bringing her back to reality.

Glancing at the speedometer, she saw the needle touching seventy-five as they approached a hairpin curve.

"Well enough," she replied, easing her foot off the gas just enough to round the curve safely. A cynical smile played at the corners of her mouth. He had invited her to drive his car, but of course he hadn't realized the extent of her inner turmoil and how great her need to somehow leave it behind was. Still, she wasn't the only person in the car, and suddenly conscious of his concern, she eased her foot off the gas, slowing the car to a more reasonable speed.

"Do you want to tell me what you were attempting to run away from at that hair-raising speed?" Tyler asked, releasing a pent-up breath and watching the needle on the speedometer move downward.

His admission to being unnerved caused the smile playing at the corners of her mouth to widen. "No."

Coming to a straight stretch of road, she accelerated, the response of the sleek car giving her a sense of power. But it was a pale substitute for the power she had lost over her life, and so she again slowed. She could feel Tyler's eyes on her, but she didn't once shift her attention away from the road.

"Why does Joe Nieley hate your former husband so much?" Tyler asked.

Her grip tightened on the wheel. The ocean lay ahead, gleaming in the last rays of the late-afternoon sun. "Toby and Joe grew up together," she said wearily, as if she had gone over this a thousand times in her mind, which in fact she had. "Joe had everything—money, brains, looks. Toby, on the other hand, had no money. He had a good mind, but not a brilliant one, and while he had a nice face, he wasn't handsome. But he was likable and that was one thing Joe lacked. From what I have been able to gather, Joe was never likable. He has always enjoyed using his wealth and influence to control others." A deep frown etched itself onto her features. "Both Joe and Toby fell in love with the same girl. Her name was Julie Hollain. She chose Joe because he could offer her more of life's luxuries. Toby left town and enlisted in the army the day before the wedding. It was the day of the wedding that Joe's hatred for Toby began. To be more specific, it was the wedding night—when he discovered that his bride wasn't as pure as he'd thought. Theirs was a generation that believed strongly that a girl should go to her husband a virgin, and Joe was a proud and conceited man. The thought that he had been tricked into taking 'secondhand' merchandise ate at him. He kept at his wife constantly until she confessed that she had been secretly seeing Toby when she was supposed to have been Joe's girl. When Toby returned to town a few years later after his stint in the military, Joe became more and more obsessed by his hatred of the man who had deflowered his wife.''

Kate paused and took a harsh breath. ''Julie didn't make things any easier,'' she went on. ''Her marriage had never been happy, and she began to hang around Toby's garage. He never reacted to any of her advances, though, and then he married me. She was furious. She came by our home one night, drunk, and made a terrible scene. That was when Toby first learned the extent of the grudge Joe held against him. She said that Toby was the only man she had ever really loved and that she had told Joe that. She also let it slip that Joe thought she and Toby had resumed their high school affair almost as soon as Toby had returned to town. Toby told her to go back to her husband and tell him the truth, but she didn't. Instead, she left town and filed for a divorce. Naturally there was a lot of gossip, and there were a few people, close friends of Julie's, who knew about her youthful affair with Toby. Behind Joe's back, they said he'd been used . . . that Julie had only married him for his money...that she had made a fool of him. It's a small town and Joe heard the talk. It fed his hatred of Toby. He tried several times to force Toby into bankruptcy. He even came by the garage once and tried to start a fight by making a pass at me.'' Kate drew another harsh breath. ''I thought that when Toby died that would be the end of it. But I guess wounded pride in a man like Joe Nieley can build a hatred that surpasses even death."

"How did Toby die?" Tyler asked when she fell silent.

"Pneumonia," she answered tersely, and then her mouth formed a hard, straight line that indicated she didn't want to talk anymore.

Respecting her unspoken wish for silence, Tyler asked no more questions.

Kate turned onto a small side road, then drove along the rocky coastline for a short distance. At last she pulled off onto the side of the road, turned off the ignition and, leaving the keys in the car, climbed out and started toward the water's edge.

Tyler retrieved the keys. After locking the car, he followed.

Scrambling over large boulders, then down a steep incline, Kate came to a small stretch of beach sandwiched between the tall, rough-edged rocks. It was perhaps ten feet wide and very private. She and Toby had discovered it years before, and she came here whenever she wanted to be alone.

Kate sat down on the sand and drew her knees up under her chin. Wrapping her arms around her legs, she stared out at the ocean as it washed against the rocks projecting into the water on each side of the flat piece of sand. She knew what she wanted to happen next. She just wasn't at all certain how to achieve it, and she did not have a great deal of time. As Tyler joined her, nervousness caused her back muscles to tighten painfully.

She chewed self-consciously on her bottom lip as she watched him lower himself to the sand. He was definitely an attractive man. She recalled the way his lips had felt when he'd kissed her and was able to assure herself that what she was about to do would not be unbearably distasteful.

Her eyes traveled over his shoulders and back. The lines of his body were easily discernible beneath his knit shirt. Noting the definition of the muscles of his arms, she guessed that he lifted weights to keep in shape.

Her gaze traveled to his legs. As she recalled the feel of their strength pressed against her, a tingling warmth mingled with the butterflies in her stomach.

Following the line of his body back to his face, she discovered him watching her, his expression shuttered.

"Why do I have the distinct feeling I'm being sized up as if I were a racehorse you're considering betting your life's savings on?" he asked.

She forced herself to smile and inject a bantering tone into her voice. "Surely you've been looked over by a woman before."

"True," he admitted, "but I knew what they wanted."

Swinging her gaze back to the ocean, she fought to keep her tone nonchalant. "I'm not so different."

"That's a 180-degree change in attitude from last night."

"I thought men expected women to change their minds," she tossed back, watching the sunlight fade into evening dusk. Her arms tightened around her legs. She was running out of time. It would take an hour to drive back to town and she would have to shower and change before meeting Joe. Running a hand through her perspiration-dampened hair, she said, "Have you ever gone skinny-dipping?"

His gaze narrowed as he studied her profile. "A couple of times."

"It's been a hot day." She got to her feet in one quick fluid movement. Standing facing him, she caught the bottom of her T-shirt and pulled it off before she lost her nerve. Letting it fall to the sand, she reached around behind her to unfasten her bra. Her trembling fingers made the task take longer than it should have.

"Would you like some help?" he offered, rising to stand in front of her.

She didn't want to say no, but she also didn't want him walking behind her and seeing her back. Forcing a smile, she made her fingers work and the bra fell free. "Thanks, but I have it," she murmured in low and what she hoped were seductive tones as she let the bra drop to the sand beside the T-shirt.

She saw his body tense as he studied the fullness of her breasts. *Don't blow it now,* she warned herself and, reaching to grasp the bottom edges of his shirt, heard herself say, "Will you join me?"

"I was considering doing just that," he replied, a husky edge entering his voice. He stood motionless as she began lifting his shirt.

Her breasts brushed seductively against his bared chest as she rose on tiptoes to slip the shirt over his head. Dropping it to the ground to join her own clothing, she looked into his face.

The dark intensity of his gaze made her knees feel strangely weak. Then he reached for her, his hands moving caressingly over her body. "You do surprise me, Kate," he murmured, cupping her breasts, then bending to kiss each hardening nipple.

"I would have thought you'd be used to women being attracted to you," she somehow managed as an unexpectedly strong sensation of pleasure spread over her.

His lips found hers. As she let her body melt against his, the rough hair on his chest brushed against her softer flesh, and a need that shocked her by its power began to grow. Soon the rest of their clothing joined what was already on the ground.

He knew how to touch a woman, and for the first time she knew the sensation of desperately wanting a man.

But as he laid her gently back on the sand, panic suddenly threatened. Swallowing it back, she closed her eyes and told herself she was doing this for Toby.

Her teeth closed over her bottom lip, holding back a cry of pain and shock as he possessed her. After an initial look of surprise, he resumed his lovemaking, rekindling her desire and expertly bringing her body to a level of excitement and pleasure she had never before known.

Afterward she lay looking up at the first stars to light the night sky while the sound of the ocean filled her ears. She could feel him watching her and her muscles tightened. At last, shifting into a sitting position, she reached for her clothes.

Rising to his feet in a single motion, Tyler caught Kate by her upper arms and lifted her to her feet. Holding her captive in front of him, he growled, "I want to know what's going on!"

The anger etched into his features unnerved her. Still, she managed to maintain a cool composure. "We are having a brief encounter."

He shook her once, his anger riding a fine edge of control. "Don't play games with me! You were a virgin."

She tried to jerk free. "I was hoping you wouldn't notice."

"You were married." His voice was low and puzzled.

Regarding him in icy silence, she again tried to pull away.

His fingers dug deeper. "I want an explanation!"

The coldness in her eyes spread through her body. "Toby was injured in the military. He wasn't capable...." She let her words drift away.

Drawing a sharp breath, Tyler practically lifted her off her feet as he brought their faces closer together. "Why me?"

"You're hurting me," she hissed in response, again struggling to gain her freedom.

Grudgingly he relaxed his hold, but he didn't free her. "I want an answer. Why was I given the questionable privilege of deflowering you, as you like to put it?"

Time was passing and Kate had to get home. Deciding that honesty was best, she said tightly, "Because it would mean nothing to you. I expect you to leave town early tomorrow and never return. Now let go of me!"

This time he did as requested.

The way he was looking at her made her feel suddenly embarrassed and vulnerable. Grabbing her clothes, she backed into the deep shadows of the rocks and dressed quickly.

As she slipped on her shoes, she glanced toward him to find him pulling on his shirt. "I'll meet you at the car," she said, starting toward the rocky incline.

"No, you won't." Catching her by the arm, he jerked her to a halt. "I haven't finished with my questions."

She faced him defiantly. "You have all the answers you're going to get."

His narrow gaze raked her. "This has something to do with Joe Nieley."

"But it has nothing to do with you!" she snarled. "Now let go of me."

Ignoring her demand, he continued to regard her darkly. "Yesterday you made it clear you were not interested in marrying the man. This morning you didn't even want to share a picnic basket with him. But this afternoon you seduced me, obviously to protect your former husband's secret. That leads me to believe that Joe Nieley must have a pretty powerful hold over you—one he has decided to use to force you to marry him."

She stood perfectly straight and met his speculation with cold silence.

"I want to know what hold he has over you," Tyler demanded.

Her jaw tensed. "I have to be getting back home. And I think it would be best if you packed and left tonight."

He stood like a granite wall blocking her escape. "You are not going anywhere until I get an answer."

Panic again threatened. If she didn't get back soon, Joe was certain to suspect something, and she was afraid of what he would do. He wasn't rational where his hatred of Toby was concerned. "It's money," she said at last. "My mother borrowed a large sum from Joe several years ago without my knowledge, and she has borrowed smaller sums since then. Either I marry him, or he'll call in the debt immediately."

"How much?" Tyler's tone was clipped.

"Forty-seven thousand four hundred and eleven dollars," she recited. Then she added acidly, "I suppose I should be flattered to know that I'm worth almost as much as a Porsche. Now let go of me. I have to be getting home."

"Not yet." His voice was a low growl as he drew a harsh breath. "I'll give you the money."

"You'll what?" She stared at him incredulously.

"I will give you the money," he repeated in a cold level voice.

She hesitated only a moment. "I'll pay you back, every cent plus interest," she promised, barely able to believe his offer.

"What you will do is marry me."

Her eyes widened. She felt as if she was suddenly caught in a new nightmare. "You can't be serious. You can't possibly want to marry me. You don't even like me. Ever since you arrived in this town, you have chided and ridiculed me."

Releasing her, he leaned against a rock and regarded her dryly. "My father, as I mentioned before, was quite taken with you. Apparently he suspected that one day Joe Nieley was going to back you into a corner you couldn't get out of, so he decided to provide you with an alternative—me."

"I don't believe this," she muttered. That anyone could control the man in front of her to the degree that he would marry a woman he didn't want didn't seem possible.

His jaw twitched angrily. "I've spent my life working beside my father at Langston Industries. I've always assumed that control of the company would automatically pass to me. My father, however, has threatened to divide his voting stock between myself, my brother and my sister unless I marry you. But I did get him to agree that if we found we were not compatible, the marriage has to last only two years. Therefore, what I am proposing is a two-year arrangement between us. During those two years, I will provide you with a monthly allowance, say, four thousand dollars. That should cover what you will need to send to your mother plus give you money to save or spend as you wish. I will also provide you with a large settlement sum at the time of the divorce. That should enable you to begin a new life."

"You're serious," she breathed, staring at him.

"I want control of Langston Industries and you want control of your life," he said tersely. "To gain these ends, all we have to do is convince my father that we're trying to make our marriage work." The frown on his face deepened. "That will mean we will have to share a bed. My father will expect both of us to be faithful to our wedding vows and I am not a celibate type of man. Toward the end of the second year, you and I will begin to argue. Once the set time limit has passed, we can stage a major disagreement and dissolve the union. It's a better deal than what Joe Nieley is offering."

"True," she agreed, wondering if this was real or merely a hallucination created by the strain she was under.

Picking up his shoes, he pulled them on, then returned his attention to her. "May I assume we have an agreement?"

"I . . ." She thought of refusing. Tyler Langston frightened her. Then she considered the alternative and heard herself say in firm tones, "Yes, we have an agreement."

Nodding, he motioned for her to precede him and then followed as she climbed up the rocky incline and made her way back to the car.

"I'll drive this time," he said, climbing in behind the wheel.

She settled in the passenger seat, then watched the passing landscape as he took the road at a safer pace than she had. The day didn't seem real. Nothing seemed real. She was being given a chance to escape . . . one she would never have dreamed of in a million years. Glancing at Tyler, she noted the taut line of his jaw and was reminded of a bear caught in a trap. *Join the crowd,* she thought acidly. *I've been in that trap most of my life.*

JOE WAS WAITING on the porch when they arrived at the house. "Your mother tried to tell me that you were exhausted from overwork and that she had left you sleeping," he said to Kate contemptuously as she and

Tyler started up the steps toward him. "But Harriet was never any good at lying."

His expression was an open declaration of war. As a vivid burst of red stars filled the night sky accompanied by a tremendous bang, Kate couldn't help thinking that the fireworks display was a perfect backdrop for this encounter.

"Contrary to what you're implying," Tyler said coldly, "what my fiancée does with her time is none of your business."

Disbelief mingled with outrage on Joe's face. "*Your* fiancée?"

"Yes, *my* fiancée," Tyler confirmed.

Joe's gaze swung to Kate and his tone became threatening. "If you think—"

Tyler cut Joe short, his voice ice. "What my fiancée thinks is also none of your business," he snapped. "However, you and I do have some business to conduct. Kate told me about her mother's debt to you and I want the papers for the repayment of that loan drawn up and ready for me to pick up and send to my lawyer by ten tomorrow morning."

Joe's complexion was turning purple. "You cannot order me around!"

Tyler's eyes narrowed dangerously. "What you tried to do to Kate was, to say the least, unethical. If you give me any trouble or if you give Kate or her family any further trouble, I will mention your name to a few friends of mine in the financial community at the federal level. In fact, that would probably be a good idea either way. No man should be allowed to use his power and wealth to force others to do his bidding.'' The hint of a derisive smile curled a corner of Tyler's mouth. "I wouldn't be surprised if an investigation of your practices didn't turn up several incidences of unethical, if not illegal, behavior.''

Joe's face contorted into an ugly expression of anger on the narrow edge of control. "I don't like being threatened.''

"No one does,'' Tyler said, glancing at Kate.

Kate was shocked by the note of fear that had crept from behind Joe's rage as he and Tyler faced each other in a challenging silence. She had never known him to be afraid of anyone. He was too wrapped up in his self-conceit to believe he could be harmed.

Glancing back at her questionable champion, she felt his cold command and realized just how powerful an opponent Tyler Langston could be.

Suddenly Joe expelled a harsh breath, almost a snarl, and stalked past them off the porch and down the street.

"Your Mr. Nieley,'' said Tyler to Kate, "strikes me as the kind of man who'll only pick on those he considers reasonably defenseless and won't risk his own destruction even for revenge. Still, a person can never be certain about the actions of others.'' He frowned, watching Joe's retreating back. "He does have the very self-destructive weakness of allowing his emotions to rule his actions.''

"A weakness you would never exhibit," Kate mused, studying the taut line of Tyler Langston's jaw.

The hint of a derisive smile added a cutting edge to his expression. "We all have our weaknesses. I just hide mine better." The hint of the smile vanished as he added with cold command, "I think it would be wise to resettle your mother and the twins in a new location as soon as possible."

"It's so comforting to know that you don't believe in someone using his wealth and power to force others to do his bidding," Kate noted sarcastically.

He glared at her, and the coldness in the brown depths of his eyes made her shiver. "The agreement we have will be as advantageous to you as it will be to me. Of course, if you prefer continuing to negotiate with Joe Nieley...." He left the sentence open, pausing to give her a chance to respond.

She scowled. "You know that would be impossible now."

"It would have been impossible even if I hadn't appeared on the scene," he corrected her curtly.

"You're right," she admitted grudgingly. Just the thought of Joe touching her caused her skin to crawl.

"As for moving your mother and the twins, I was thinking of their comfort and well-being. You might also look upon such a move as a preventative measure to safeguard your future," he continued dryly.

Again she was forced to admit that he had made two very valid points. Joe was in a rage, and when he was that way there was no predicting what he might do to cause trouble. Then there was her mother's gullibility. She didn't want to end her two-year arrangement with Tyler only to find that Joe had somehow managed to again ensnare her by using her mother or the twins. "My mother has a sister in Ohio she is very fond of. Periodically she has mentioned a desire to move closer to her," she said tightly.

"I will arrange for the move to take place as soon as possible," Tyler said, adding, "Consider it a gratuity."

Kate's back stiffened with pride. They had a business arrangement. She wanted no favors from him. "You will keep track of what the move costs, and when this house and the garage are sold, I will repay you. If the sale doesn't bring enough to cover all of the expenses, I will pay you the rest out of..." She hesitated, unable to make herself say the word allowance. "Out of my salary for playing the part of your wife," she finally concluded.

"Loving wife," he corrected darkly. "No one but ourselves and my father are to know about my agreement with him regarding my marriage to you. And, I repeat, my father has to believe we are honestly trying to make our marriage work. In fact, for the sake of our peace of mind, it would be best if he thought we were strongly attracted to one another. That will save both of us from a great deal of paternal counseling."

She had no desire to become known as a person who could be purchased if the price was right. She was having a hard enough time reconciling herself to the situation. Nodding her agreement, she went inside and up to her room.

A few minutes later as she stood in the shower, she told herself she had to think of her relationship with Tyler Langston strictly as a business agreement. The problem there was that sharing the man's bed added a very unbusinesslike flavor to the arrangement.

Even more distressing was the fact that, under the circumstances, sharing Tyler Langston's bed should have been at least a nuisance and at most a distasteful obligation. Instead, the thought brought a chill of wanton excitement.

"It's just that sex is so very new to me and he's so very good at it," she muttered, attempting to justify her attitude to herself. Then her very practical side came to her rescue. Obviously it was better to be facing the prospect with interest than with distaste.

"I simply have to start thinking of myself as a modern liberated woman," she mused aloud. "Under those conditions, I should be able to see a little unemotionally involved sex as an interesting way to pass an otherwise dull evening."

But as she climbed out of the shower, the gray eyes that stared back at her from the image in the mirror were skeptical.

"I'M VERY HAPPY for the both of you," Harriet said, her gaze traveling dubiously from her daughter to Tyler and then back to Kate as she sank onto one of the kitchen chairs. "But I hope you won't be offended if

I say I'm rather surprised. The two of you didn't seem to be getting along all that well."

"I admit that the feathers flew at first," Tyler said, slipping a possessive arm around Kate's shoulder, "but once we took some time to get to know one another, I saw that my father was right."

"Your father?" Harriet asked.

"He was the reason I came up here," Tyler said, his hand applying a small but definitive amount of pressure on Kate's arm to remind her to keep smiling and stifle any sarcastic remarks that might come dancing onto the tip of her tongue. "He was very taken with Kate and informed me in no uncertain terms that he felt she would make the perfect wife for me. After listening to him rave about her for two weeks I decided that the only way I was ever going to have any peace was to come up here and see for myself."

"I did realize that Uriah was fond of Kate," Harriet mused, the smile she was forcing on her mouth only serving to emphasize the anxiety building in her eyes. "And I do hope the two of you will be very happy."

Glancing at Tyler, Kate could tell that he, too, knew that her mother was near the brink of panic worrying about what was going to happen to her and the twins once their primary source of income was gone. But his return glance told Kate that he was leaving up to her the decision of when to inform Harriet of the plans for her and the twins. Despite her anger at her mother for placing her in such a vulnerable position, Kate and

Harriet had been through too much together for Kate to enjoy watching her mother's growing discomfort. "I don't like the idea of leaving you and the twins alone up here in Maine," she said levelly. "I've been thinking it would be a good idea if you lived nearer Aunt Andrea."

"That is a nice thought." Harriet frowned wistfully. "And Andrea has always said that she would love to have me work for her as a seamstress." Her gaze traveled to Tyler, and she added, "My sister owns a small but very exclusive dress shop." Then shaking her head, she turned her attention back to Kate. "But I'm afraid the move would be too expensive. I'll have to find some sort of work here."

"Tyler has volunteered to lend us the money for the move. We can pay him back when we sell this house and the garage." As she spoke, Kate fought back the unpleasant edge that threatened to creep into her voice.

"He has?" Harriet looked questioningly at Tyler.

"I want my new bride to be able to concentrate on me and not be constantly worrying about her family," he said reassuringly.

A genuine smile spread over Harriet's face. "I've always hated being so far from Andrea."

"Then it's settled." Tyler's voice took on an air of command. "Tuesday, Kate and I will apply for our license." Focusing his attention on Harriet, he said, "I'd appreciate it if, while we're doing that, you'd make the arrangements for a small wedding to take place in this house, one week from today. All we'll need is a minister and a few flowers. Then on Wednesday, you, Kate and the twins will fly out to Ohio and find you a new home. Meanwhile, I'll have one of my legal staff come up here and arrange for the sale of the house and garage.''

''I . . . I'll need some time to find a dress,'' Kate stammered, feeling as if she had been suddenly caught up in a whirlwind. No, a tornado, she thought, considering the man beside her.

''I'm certain your Aunt Andrea will have something suitable,'' he countered, catching her by the chin and tilting her face upward so that she could read the uncompromising command in his eyes. ''We do want to begin our life together as soon as possible.''

''Yes,'' she replied from behind her plastic smile. She knew he was thinking that the sooner they began, the sooner their arrangement would be over.

''Now, if you ladies will excuse me, I have a couple of phone calls to make, and then I'm going to bed. It's been a long day.'' Kissing Kate lightly on the lips, as if placing a final seal on their bargain, he smiled at Harriet and left the room.

''I honestly can't believe any of this!'' Harriet said, breaking the sudden silence that filled the kitchen as the two women watched his retreating back. Harriet chattered excitedly for several minutes, expressing her surprise further and sharing her delight at the idea of moving near her sister. Then, rising from her chair, she gave her daughter a hug. ''I never dreamed you would be so lucky as to catch a man like Tyler Langston, with his family connections and wealth.''

''Me neither,'' Kate muttered, the cynical edge in her voice going unnoticed as her motner continued to marvel at her good fortune. Needing to be alone, Kate said tiredly, ''It's been a long day for me, too, and it looks as if tomorrow is going to be even more hectic. I think I should be going to bed also.'' She disentangled herself from her mother's embrace and left the room.

''Good night, dear,'' Kate heard her mother call out as she reached the top of the stairs. She paused to stare at Tyler's closed door—apparently he'd finished his phone calls—feeling more and more uneasy about their arrangement with each passing moment. Though their touch had been light, the feel of his lips continued to linger warmly on hers. Frowning, she reminded herself that he was more anxious for their marriage to end than to begin, and she assured herself curtly that she felt the same way. Abruptly she wiped her lips with the palm of her hand to rid herself of the disquieting sensation and went into her room, closing the door behind her.

Exhausted, she changed for bed and climbed under the covers. But just as she was finally drifting into a restless sleep, a hesitant knock sounded on her door.

''Kate,'' Harriet said from the other side of the barrier, ''I need to talk to you.''

Turning on the bedside light, Kate dragged herself to a sitting position. "Couldn't this wait until morning?" she asked as her mother opened the door.

Harriet looked tense and anxious. "No," she replied, shaking her head firmly. She began to pace the room, wringing her hands agitatedly in front of her. "I honestly don't know how to tell you this," she said at last in deeply apologetic tones. "You've carried so many burdens that should never have been yours. But I feel I must tell you since you'll probably find out about it anyway."

"Go on, then, Mom," Kate said, sinking tiredly back against the pillows and wondering if she could face any more problems.

"It concerns Joe Nieley," Harriet said hesitantly. "You know what a temper he has, and he's going to be furious when he finds out about your engagement."

Guessing what was coming next, Kate fought to cover an intense wave of hostility toward her mother. What would be the point of giving vent to her temper now? And, she thought cynically, she didn't want to be accused of being one of those weak-willed types who let emotions rule their behavior. Aloud she said stiffly, "Joe already knows."

Harriet froze in her pacing and turned to face her daughter. "How did he take it?"

"Badly, as you would expect," Kate replied tersely.

"I was afraid of that." Harriet began pacing again. "I never told you this and I know I should never have done it, but I borrowed money from him. There was your father's funeral to pay for, and John's drinking and gambling left us with a lot of debts. Then there were the twins' hospital bills. I took a second mortgage out on the house but even that wasn't enough.'' Worry etched itself even more deeply into the lines of her face as she again stopped her pacing and stood facing Kate. ''Anyway, I'm certain Joe will demand to be paid immediately, considering your impending marriage and our leaving town. And that will take most if not all of the money from the sale of the house and garage. There won't be much, if anything, left for you to use to repay Tyler.''

After a moment's hesitation, Harriet went on, ''I...I'm sure Tyler loves you, but there is a lot of money involved...'' Harriet again hesitated, her expression one of great anguish. ''Oh, Kate,'' she said at last, ''I would hate to see your marriage start off with that kind of strain between the two of you, and it's all my fault....''

Kate's bitterness became mixed with compassion. Despite the fact that she had become a sort of collateral, thanks to her mother's borrowing, it really wasn't Harriet's fault—she'd only done what she'd felt she had to. Gently Kate said, ''You don't have to worry about the money you owe Joe. Tyler will take care of that, too.''

Then, feeling like a piece of merchandise that had been placed on the auction block and sold to the highest bidder, Kate again felt a surge of anger. Stifling it, she said tightly, "I really am very tired and I need sleep. But before you leave, I want your promise that you will have nothing further to do with Joe Nieley and that you will never again borrow money without telling me first."

"You have my promise," Harriet assured her. She moved to the bedside and, cupping Kate's face in her hands, looked into her daughter's tired face. "I know I have never said it, but I am so sorry for all you've had to endure in your life. You deserve happiness more than anyone else I know, and I wish you all the very best with Tyler. It's about time that the Fates smiled on you."

Kate's expression remained shuttered until her mother had left the room. But as the door clicked shut, the mask fell away, exposing the bitterness beneath. *I wouldn't call my marriage to Tyler one that the Fates were smiling upon, unless they have a warped sense of humor,* she mused acidly. Then, pulling the covers around her, she muttered cynically, "Of course that is a distinct possibility, considering the paths my life has been forced to take."

# CHAPTER FOUR

"YOU LOOK VERY NICE TODAY," Tyler commented, breaking the silence that filled the Porsche as, one week later, they drove southward down the Maine coast as Mr. and Mrs. Tyler Langston.

"Thank you," Kate murmured. A small cynical smile quirked her mouth as she noted that this was the first truly personal remark he had made to her since his reappearance that afternoon for the wedding ceremony.

Until then, she had not seen him or spoken to him since the day they had applied for their license. Their only communication had been a message, delivered to her upon her return from Ohio by the person he had left in charge of selling her garage and her mother's home, instructing her to have her things packed and ready to be picked up the afternoon of the wedding.

She was certain that even while Tyler had continued with the arrangements regarding their union, he had been trying to find a way out of going through with the marriage. Obviously, he'd failed.

During the ceremony she had felt like an actress caught up in the middle of a play, with all the characters behaving much as the audience would have expected. The twins had twittered, her mother had wept, and Uriah, chauffeured up for the event, had beamed. Even the kiss at the end of the ceremony had felt unreal.

"Are you going to let me in on the joke?" Tyler asked now.

"Joke?" She frowned, glancing toward him questioningly.

"The one that brought that odd little smile to your face a moment ago," he elaborated.

Her frown deepened. "I was thinking that we were the only two people at the ceremony today who weren't getting what we wanted," she replied honestly. "Your father was seeing you marry the woman he had personally chosen for you and my mother is being given the opportunity to live near her sister."

Tyler's jaw hardened. "You have to learn to look at the long-term picture. In two years you will be free, with a financial cushion that will enable you to start a new life, and my agreement with my father will eventually give me control of Langston Industries."

"And everyone will live happily ever after," she muttered.

"Yes," he growled, anger etching itself into his features. "And I would like to point out that there are many women who would not look upon two years of marriage to me as a punishment. You'll have more money at your disposal than you've ever had in your life or could have ever hoped to have. You'll have servants to cater to your every wish and—" he glanced at her dryly "—I could have sworn you enjoyed our lovemaking last week on the beach."

"It isn't being married to you that bothers me," she defended curtly as a flush darkened her cheeks at the memory of their intimate encounter. "It's the circumstances surrounding the marriage."

He scowled. "Because you were forced into it? Because I was the lesser of two evils?"

"Because we were both forced into it. Because it was something that neither of us would have chosen," she pointed out bitterly.

He glanced her way again, his expression grim. "Be that as it may, it's a fait accompli and I suggest that we both try to make the best of it."

"Agreed," she said.

Once more a silence fell over the interior of the car.

Surreptitiously studying Tyler's profile, Kate felt her stomach knot. She was married to a man who was practically a stranger and was on her way to a totally alien environment. The Langston family was part of Bostonian upper society. Looking down at her work-roughened hands, she wondered how she was going to fit into his life even for two years.

The continuing silence in the car only added to her tenseness. "You haven't told me where we are going," she said, forcing a conversational tone into her voice.

"I arranged to have some time away from the office. We're going to New York" was his clipped response.

New York. A part of her was relieved they weren't going directly to Boston, but it had been a hectic week and the thought of facing one of the busiest cities in the world didn't appeal to her, either.

"I would have preferred to take you to Paris," he continued, his attention remaining on the road ahead as a grimness entered his voice. "But my brother, Ross, is in Texas at the moment, attempting to head our Houston branch, and I need to be where I can get there fast in case of trouble."

"You make it sound as if you expect a catastrophe," Kate observed, recalling that Ross, along with his sister, stood to benefit if Tyler's marriage did not last the required two years.

"My brother has absolutely no interest in our company, except for the money it brings in. My father, however, is determined to spark his interest by placing him in positions of responsibility. The fallacy in that ploy is that my younger brother has no sense of responsibility to begin with. So he spends his time nightclubbing and carousing and paying as little attention to business as possible. And I spend at least one month out of every year cleaning up the messes his childish behavior creates."

"Maybe he's simply not cut out to be a businessman," Kate said in defence of the brother who was not there to defend himself. "Maybe he's the creative type."

A cynical smile played across Tyler's face. "As long as he has a luxury apartment to live in and a fast car to drive, he'd be willing to play at anything you might want to suggest.''

''And maybe your expectations of people are too high,'' she said, forgetting Ross momentarily and wondering again how she was going to fit into Tyler's world.

Tyler's gaze flicked at her. ''Maybe,'' he muttered grimly. After a moment, he said, ''However, in Ross's case I'd settle for just a glimmer of adult behavior. He was only four years old when our mother died, and being the baby of the family, he was badly spoiled after that. But he's twenty-six now, and it's time he grew up.''

The fact that he had offered some excuse for his brother caused Kate to study the profile of the man behind the wheel more closely. He was human after all, she concluded, seeing the frustration behind the irritation, and she found herself feeling a certain camaraderie with him. If anyone knew what it was like to be caught up in near disasters created by a family member, it was she, and Kate could sympathize with anyone else caught in the same trap.

She leaned back in her seat and returned her attention to the road. As she recalled that their destination was New York, her back muscles tensed painfully. She felt a strong need to go somewhere where it was quiet, where she could have a few days to unwind and adjust to this new, albeit temporary, life in front of her. ''I was wondering,'' she said carefully, ''if it would be possible for us to find a place on a beach or in the mountains for a few days of peace and quiet.'' The glance he sent her brought a scarlet flush to her cheeks, and she added tightly, ''This may have been a typical week for you, but for me it's been exhausting. I'm having a difficult time even remembering what day of the week it is.''

''It's Sunday,'' he informed her, ''and though there is nothing I would rather do than to spend a few quiet days with you, we are going to New York for a purpose. That suit you have on is probably the only decent piece of clothing you own.''

The sympathy she had been feeling for the man vanished. ''My clothes might not be expensive, but they're presentable,'' she defended curtly.

''I'm sorry. I didn't mean that the way it sounded.''

Surprised by his apology but not appeased, she regarded him frostily. ''What did you mean?''

Raking a hand through his hair, he said, ''Your clothes are fine for the society in which you've traveled. But in the society in which you're going to travel for the next two years, designer labels are important—along with shoes and purses to match each outfit and a different outfit for every occasion. You will also need a few pieces of good jewelry. You are my wife, and I expect you to look and act the part.''

''Maybe you would like me to take a few elocution lessons and perhaps a course in table manners,'' she suggested acidly.

The hint of a smile played at the corners of his mouth. ''Luckily you somehow managed to escape having a strong New England accent, and your table manners appear to be adequate. I've noticed that you use a knife and fork properly and you don't slurp your soup.''

She was about to tell him what she thought of his superior attitude when an underlying inflection in his voice caused her to study him more closely. His smile, though derisive, was self-directed. He was ridiculing his own snobbery! Drawing a terse breath, she again sat back in her seat and stared at the road ahead. Tyler Langston was not going to be an easy man to get to know. But what really bothered her was that she was beginning to *want* to know him.

THEY WERE IN MASSACHUSETTS when dusk began to fall.

''We're still three to four hours out of New York,'' Tyler said with a yawn. ''I'm too tired to drive much longer and I don't think my nerves could take your driving, so I suggest we stop for the night.''

Kate, who was beginning to feel as if she were a part of the seat, ignored his comment about her driving and nodded in agreement.

Pulling off the interstate, he checked them into a motel room, and after unloading their luggage, they went into the attached restaurant to eat.

Families with young children who complained and squirmed in their chairs, an older couple looking satisfied with life and apparently enjoying the activity around them, a couple of truckers talking business, and a young couple obviously on their honeymoon filled the tables surrounding Kate and Tyler, but Kate didn't notice any of them. A subject she had forced to remain at the back of her mind all day now demanded her undivided attention. This was her wedding night. Looking across the table, she watched Tyler drinking his coffee and wondered what to expect.

"You're staring," he said, meeting her nervous gaze with a shuttered mask. "You needn't worry. I'm not the big bad wolf. I won't devour you."

"I didn't think you would," she muttered, fighting her embarrassment at being so obvious. Then, returning her attention to her food, she ate without tasting. Tyler Langston intimidated her, and she didn't like the sensation. And yet...she could not deny a deep stirring of excitement and expectation about what the night might hold.

Back in their room, he behaved almost as if he was indifferent to her presence. "You can shower first," he said, pocketing a pack of cigarettes. "I'm going to take a walk. I'm still stiff from driving."

As the door closed behind him, a frown replaced the schooled coolness of her features. Wedding nights, she mused, at least in her case, were not all they were purported to be.

Opening her suitcase, she took out a burnished rose silk and lace floor-length nightgown. "Sexy but elegant" was how her aunt had described it. A matching robe with bell-style sleeves accompanied it. Kate would never have purchased such extravagant night-wear, but it had been a gift from Aunt Andrea, and after Tyler's earlier remarks regarding her clothing, she was grateful that her aunt had insisted on this particular wedding present.

"Providing he even notices," she muttered as she carried the gown and robe into the bathroom.

Tyler was sitting in a chair reading when she came out.

Seeing her, his eyes narrowed with interest. "Just some little thing you had lying around?" he asked dryly.

"Just some little thing my aunt thought you might appreciate," she replied tightly, suddenly wishing she had chosen to wear one of her long cotton night-gowns instead. She knew she looked like an open invitation. Under other circumstances that would have been fine, but under the circumstances of their relationship, she felt acutely wanton.

Rising from the chair, he picked up his robe and shaving kit. As he started toward the bathroom, he paused in front of her. "I do," he murmured as he traced the line of her jaw with the tips of his fingers. Placing a light promising kiss on her lips, he went into the bathroom.

Furious and embarrassed that she had placed herself in the position of making the first move toward the more intimate side of their arrangement, she paced the room. He had to think she had a strong wanton streak in her, and as much as she hated to admit it, she did care what he thought about her. Momentarily she considered changing into something less provocative but vetoed that idea, deciding it was too late to do that. Instead she settled on being asleep when he came out of the bathroom.

But as exhausted as she was, sleep didn't come as easily as she had hoped. To her dismay, she was still awake when she heard the knob on the bathroom door turning. She shifted onto her side so that her back was toward that end of the room, and the other half of the bed, and feigned sleep.

Turning off the lights, Tyler climbed into the bed. At first she thought he had bought her act, but as he rolled over onto his side, placing his back toward hers, he said quietly, "Good night, Kate," in a voice that left no doubt he knew she was still awake.

Darn the man! She felt insulted from the tips of her toes to the hair on her head. Grudgingly she admitted to herself that she'd expected, perhaps even anticipated, more aggressive behavior from him. That he found her so undesirable that he wasn't even willing to make the first move came as an ego-crushing blow. Schooling her voice into a tone of indifference, she muttered a good-night in return and ordered herself to go to sleep. But sleep was still elusive, and she heard Tyler snoring gently for what seemed like hours before she dozed off. Her final thought was to wonder if he had changed his mind about the intimate side of their arrangement and had decided to maintain a mistress instead. *If that's what he wants,* she told herself angrily, *it's fine with me.*

"GOOD MORNING, KATE," a male voice said softly. She awoke slowly to the feel of strong arms around her and warm lips trailing kisses along the sensitive cords at the back of her neck. "I hope you're well rested because, while I am a patient man, I do have my limits, and you are much too soft and inviting to resist any longer," Tyler murmured huskily in her ear.

"You didn't have any trouble last night," she muttered, sharply recalling the insult she had felt.

"Last night I was being thoughtful," he said, turning her onto her back and levering himself on an elbow so that he could look down into her face. "I knew you were exhausted, and your nerves seemed to be frayed." His eyes darkened with purpose. "But I do intend to consummate this marriage. That was part of our agreement."

His free hand was moving in leisurely exploration along her body, leaving a trail of fire in its wake. "I remember," she said in low, throaty tones, shocked by the intensity of her reaction to his touch.

"Good," he growled against her lips as he claimed her mouth in a demand for possession that sent her blood raging through her veins.

Later, as she lay beside him, she could not fault his lovemaking in any way. He had never forgotten that there were two people involved.

"You must have had a great deal of practice," she mused, smiling softly and running her fingers over the hard, warm surface of his chest. "You're very good at making love."

Levering himself up on an elbow, he smiled down at her. "It's very easy with you. You have a beautiful body."

Suddenly Kate had to fight to keep the smile on her face. Her body... He hadn't seen....

Dropping a kiss on her shoulder, he said in low gruff tones, "I would love to linger here with you all day, but we have to be on our way. We only have a week in New York before I have to be back in Boston." Slipping out of bed, he picked up his shaving kit and headed toward the bathroom. "Why don't you order us some breakfast while I shave?" he suggested over his shoulder, adding just before he closed the door between them, "I'll have scrambled eggs, bacon, coffee, toast and half a grapefruit."

When she was alone in the room, the words "beautiful body" played over and over in Kate's mind as she quickly slipped back into her nightgown before calling in their breakfast order.

Theirs was a very shallow relationship based solely on self-interests, she reminded herself as she gathered her clothes together and waited for Tyler to come out of the bathroom. That her body might not be as perfect as he thought shouldn't really matter. Still, the tension his words had caused multiplied. She found herself recalling the little plaque she had seen inside his shaving kit. No doubt Linda had an unflawed body....

Their breakfast arrived just as Tyler came out of the bathroom. As they ate and made polite conversation about the weather and the drive ahead, Kate tried to relax. But she couldn't. There were too many conflicting emotions boiling inside her.

Excusing herself after eating only half a slice of toast, she picked up her clothes and started toward the bathroom. As she passed his shaving kit, her gaze locked onto it, and she found herself wondering if it was the one "Linda" had given him. Her jaw hardened, and telling herself that the woman didn't matter, she continued into the bathroom.

When she emerged a little later, Tyler had finished his breakfast and was in a decidedly cool mood. She sensed he was only reacting to her, but still she couldn't relax.

The drive to New York was accomplished in heavy silence.

After they checked into their hotel room, Tyler informed Kate that he had arranged for tickets to a popular Broadway show. "You'll need something to wear," he finished in an irritated tone, as if he was beginning to consider her a nuisance. Then, without waiting for a response, he took her by the arm, led her out of the hotel and hailed a taxi.

A few minutes later she found herself in the dress department of one of the most expensive stores on Fifth Avenue. The saleswoman was much more helpful than Kate would have liked. In addition to popping in and out of the dressing room with a fresh armload of dresses every few minutes, she was constantly offering her assistance with buttons and zippers. This constant invasion of her privacy set Kate's already raw nerves on edge.

It also didn't help her mood to see the way the other saleswomen, as well as some of the shoppers, looked Tyler over with interest, as if they were considering buying him and taking him home.

Finally she found an off-the-shoulder burgundy cocktail dress with a handkerchief layered skirt of which both she and Tyler approved. Shopping for matching shoes and a purse came next. Then he insisted on purchasing a necklace, earrings and a gem-studded cocktail ring to complete the ensemble.

By the time they returned to the hotel, Kate's nerves were as tight as bowstrings. While Tyler had maintained a polite facade during their shopping expedition, she had felt the cold between them building to the level of an Arctic chill.

As they entered their hotel room loaded down with packages, he said harshly, his polite mask falling away, "Most women would have enjoyed a shopping spree like the one I've just taken you on."

"I'm just not used to spending so much money on clothes or wearing jewelry that costs more than some cars." She avoided his eyes by devoting her attention to unpacking her new dress and carefully hanging it in the closet.

Breaching the distance between them in long angry strides, he turned her toward him, his fingers closing viselike around her upper arms. "I want to know what is going on," he demanded grimly. "This cool withdrawal of yours didn't start with the purchase of that dress. It started this morning while I was shaving. When I went into the bathroom, you were smiling. When I came out, you were as nervous as a cat and exhibited the warmth of an ice cube. What happened? Did you suddenly begin to feel guilty? Did your precious Toby come back into your mind and make you feel as if you were somehow betraying him by enjoying yourself with me?"

"Toby has nothing to do with this," she managed levelly.

"Don't lie to me, Kate!" His hands tightened on her arms. "He has everything to do with this. You seduced me, a man who was practically a total stranger to you, in order to protect Toby's secret. It's obvious you loved him very much—and still do!"

In spite of her efforts to hide it, fear glistened in Kate's eyes. "You're hurting me," she said, attempting to pull free.

Looking at his hands as if only then realizing that he was even touching her, Tyler immediately released his hold. "Sorry," he said in stiff apology as she backed away. "I hope you will forgive my loss of temper." He raked a hand through his hair, embarrassment and remorse mingling in his features as he watched her rubbing her arms. "I didn't mean to hurt you. I usually keep my temper under better control. I'm just finding it a little difficult to live with a ghost. In the past, I have always made it a point to avoid becoming involved with women who are emotionally committed to other men.''

His obvious remorse made her heart stop its wild pounding. As she drew a deep breath, she realized that her arms were not really hurting. It was the fear of being hurt that had caused her overreaction. ''You didn't hurt me really,'' she murmured, adding in level tones, ''and Toby, though I cared about him very much, has nothing to do with us.'' Then, unable to continue to face Tyler, she turned away and crossed the room to stand staring out the window at the park.

''Kate,'' Tyler said, breaking the silence that threatened to settle over the room. There was an edge of impatient anger slipping out from behind his carefully controlled, reasonable tones. ''It's going to be a long two years if we don't settle whatever it is that's bothering you.''

''I know,'' she replied, her voice barely above a whisper. She was deeply embarrassed, in a way she had never been before. With her back still toward him, she said in a stronger voice, ''This is very difficult for me. I know you are used to the very best . . . that you have never had to settle for anything less than perfect—until you were forced into this marriage.''

Closing the curtains, she remained with her back toward him as she unfastened her dress and let it fall to the floor. Then, removing her slip, she laid it on the chair beside her. Next she lowered her panties to give him a full view of her lower back and buttocks, an expanse of skin crisscrossed by thin vicious-looking scars. After a moment, she quickly pulled up her panties and retrieved her slip.

"How?" he demanded gruffly.

Not wanting to see the revulsion behind his concern, she avoided his eyes as she found her robe and put it on. Holding it tightly around her body as if warding off a chill, she returned to the window, opened the curtain and again stared down at the park across the street.

"How did it happen?" he demanded again.

"My father used to beat me when he was drunk, which was most of the time," she answered woodenly.

"And your mother let him?"

"He beat her, too," she said as vivid memories caused her face to pale. "She had no one she could turn to. She was too embarrassed to tell her sister and too frightened to tell anyone else. She was afraid that my father would hear about it and beat her and me even worse."

"And so you married Toby when you were barely sixteen to escape from your father," Tyler surmised with a frown.

"It would be more correct to say that Toby married me," she replied. She could feel Tyler's eyes on the back of her neck but still could not bring herself to face him. "When Toby came back from his stint in the army, he did a lot of drinking. Adjusting to his injuries was difficult, to say the least. He became one of my father's regular drinking buddies. One night my father came home roaring drunk and started to beat me. I tried to get away and fell down the stairs. I hit my head on the way down and was knocked unconscious. My father panicked. He called Toby and told him he'd found me at the foot of the stairs when he came home and asked Toby to help him get me to a hospital. But on the way there, I came to in the car, screaming for him not to hit me again.''

Kate paused to draw a deep breath, then said, ''That's how Toby found out what had been going on. He warned my father never to touch me again. My father laughed at him and told him to mind his own business and stay out of other people's domestic affairs. That was when Toby decided to make me his domestic affair, as he liked to put it.'' A tight smile played at the corners of Kate's mouth momentarily, then vanished. ''He threatened to put my father in the hospital if he didn't consent to my marriage to him. My father was a bully. He would hit a woman or a man smaller than himself, but Toby was big, and while he was normally gentle as a lamb, he could be dangerous when provoked. So my father consented. After the ceremony, Toby told my father that he also considered my mother under his protection. The marriage convinced my father that Toby meant what he said. So after that, he did his brawling in the bars instead of at home.''

Forcing herself to face Tyler, she finished apologetically, "I'm sorry that you're stuck with so much imperfection in a wife."

His expression was shuttered as he stared at her for a long moment. Then he said in dry, angry tones, "You must think I'm an exceptionally shallow man."

"No." She shook her head vigorously to add emphasis to her denial. "It's just that I know you didn't want me for a wife in the first place, and at least, if I couldn't be socially right, I could offer you physical beauty. Instead I have hideous defects, and I . . ." Unable to go on, Kate buried her face in her hands.

Tyler moved quickly toward her, reaching out to pull her hands away and tilt her tear-wet face upward to meet his gaze. "The scars don't bother me, Kate," he said. "You must believe me. I still think your body is beautiful."

Looking into the dark depths of his eyes, she saw the honesty there. The scars really didn't bother him. As relief spread through her, a small cynical voice spoke from within. *Of course, he wouldn't care,* it said in an attempt to keep the situation in the proper perspective. *You're just a warm body that will keep him satisfied until his father's bargain is met.*

A short time later, as she dressed for their evening at the theater, Kate thought again about Tyler's reaction to her body. She realized, almost with shock, how much his attitude mattered to her. It was much more than she wanted to admit.

# CHAPTER FIVE

"WE WILL BE LIVING at the family estate," Tyler said as they drove northward out of New York a week later. "It's an enormous old place originally built in the 1700s and added on to in the 1800s and 1900s. The second floor of the south wing will be our private domain. Several years ago I had a wall between two of the rooms removed to create a large master bedroom suite with a private bath. I also have a study up there and a billiard room, and there are two guest bedrooms with an adjoining bath sandwiched between. In addition to those rooms there is a fifth room. It's small and I've been using it as a catchall. If you wish, you may convert it into a private sitting room. There are several styles of furniture from different periods stored in the attic. If you don't find anything there that suits your taste, feel free to purchase something that does. I want you to feel comfortable."

"I'm certain I can find something in the attic that will suit me," she said quietly. He hadn't added "for the duration of your stay," but she knew the thought was there, and a small hard knot threatened to form in her stomach. Frowning inwardly, she turned to study the man beside her. During the past few days, he had made it very difficult for her to always keep in mind that what they had was a short-term business agreement. He had been the perfect bridegroom. He had been attentive, made interesting conversation, taken her to the most popular Broadway shows, chosen fabulous restaurants for them to dine in and treated her to shopping sprees that would have been envied by any woman.

A warm current momentarily shot through her as she recalled his insistence on beginning the second shopping spree with the purchase of undergarments, many of which were French imports.

"A woman should dress to please her husband," he had whispered in her ear when she looked questioningly at two expensive bits of lace that were supposed to be a pair of panties and a bra. "Just think what a lift it will give me when we're sitting through a boring dinner to look at you and know that beneath a sedate, very proper outer covering is a body clothed in lingerie sexy enough to turn a man's blood to hot lava."

Fighting down a threatening blush, she'd rewarded him with a "men will be boys" smile and agreed to the purchase.

From lingerie, they progressed to sports clothes and finished with a full wardrobe topped off with two evening gowns and some very elegant pieces of jewelry. She knew he was simply dressing her to fit the image she was supposed to project as his wife. Even the Broadway shows and the meals were purposeful.

The shows would provide her with topics of conversation that would produce a veneer of culture. He threw in a few museum tours for the same reason. And the meals at the various restaurants had educated her palate. Yet, during the entire time, he acted as if he was honestly enjoying himself, making her feel less like Eliza Doolittle and more like a woman whose loving husband was intent on spoiling her.

*Don't lose your perspective,* she warned herself curtly, the frown on her face unconsciously deepening. *He's merely making the best of a difficult situation and trying to educate you so that you won't embarrass him.*

"You're staring at me as if you've suddenly discovered a third eye in the middle of my forehead," Tyler said suddenly, breaking the silence.

"I'm sorry." Kate colored, shifting her attention to the view in front of her as she admitted, "I'm more than a little nervous. I'm not certain if I can fit into your world."

"You'll fit in fine," he assured her. "Just be yourself. You have a natural charm."

Surprise, along with a glow of pleasure, registered on her face as her gaze swung back toward him. "I'm flattered that you think so."

"That was not flattery," he said matter-of-factly. "It was a statement of fact. Flattery is an insincere statement meant to play on a person's vanity in order to manipulate that person to one's own advantage." His countenance grew grim. "I don't like manipulating people. I prefer to deal with them on a strictly fair, reasonable basis." A bitter resentment entered his voice. "And I don't like people manipulating me."

The anger Kate had seen in him when he had explained the reason behind his proposal of marriage was again reflected on his face. Feeling stung, she sat back and stared out the window. She hadn't placed him in this trap.

The rest of the ride seemed interminable. Tyler reverted to silence, and Kate found herself growing more and more tense by the moment. Glancing covertly toward the man beside her, she doubted that their marriage would survive two months, never mind two years. His hatred at having been manipulated was too strong.

The prospect of a shorter union should have brought some relief. Instead Kate felt a shadow of regret pass over her and her tension increased. Furious with this irrational reaction, she told herself that she would be thrilled when her relationship with Tyler was over. Returning her gaze to the passing scenery, she ignored her husband for the rest of the journey.

Their destination was several miles outside Boston, and nothing Tyler had said fully prepared Kate for the sprawling estate that covered several acres. The grounds were entirely enclosed by a high stone wall. An iron gate guarded the entrance to the private road, which wound for nearly a mile through dense woods and thick hedges of rhododendrons before forming a circle in front of Langston Hall. The building itself was a massive structure three stories high, with wings spreading out on both sides from what had once been the original manor house.

As he parked the car, Tyler unexpectedly reached over and took Kate's hand in his. "I'm sorry about what I said earlier," he said. "It's just that I hate feeling I've been manipulated into a situation, even one as interesting and enjoyable as having you for a wife."

Her voice was brittle. "I could swear that this time you are attempting to flatter me."

Still holding her hand, he frowned and said, "I know you don't like being manipulated any more than I do. But together we can pull this off, and then the rest of our lives will be our own." Lifting her hand to his lips, he kissed it as if to seal their comradeship, and in spite of herself Kate felt a warm glow at the idea of the two of them against the world. Then looking past her to the house, he added dryly, "It's time to smile and look like newlyweds."

Following his line of vision, she saw the front door open, and an elderly man in a butler's uniform, followed by a younger man in the livery of a chauffeur, came out. They crossed the marble front porch and descended the short flight of steps to the drive.

"Welcome home, Mr. Tyler." The butler's greeting revealed the warmth of a long acquaintance, as Tyler moved around the car and opened Kate's door.

"Thank you, Michael," Tyler replied with a genuine smile. Then, placing an arm around Kate's shoulder as she emerged from the vehicle and stood beside him, he said, "This is my wife, Kate. Kate, this is Michael. He has been keeping Langston Hall running according to protocol since before I was born."

"Welcome to Langston Hall, Mrs. Langston." Michael executed a modified bow in Kate's direction, then added sincerely, "We have all been looking forward to your arrival."

"Thank you." Kate forced the required smile as she breathed an inward sigh of relief and mentally chided herself for reading one too many gothic novels. In spite of efforts to the contrary, during the drive, she had envisioned being met by a houseful of servants who looked down their noses at her and treated her as if she was an interloper.

Indicating the younger man, a tall, pleasant-looking fellow Kate judged to be in his mid- to late-twenties, Michael addressed Kate once more. "This is my son William. Whenever you wish to be chauffeured anywhere, he will be happy to drive you."

"Pleased to have you here, Mrs. Langston." William substituted a polite smile and a nod in place of his father's more formal half bow as he greeted Kate. Turning toward Tyler he said, "And it's good to have you home, sir."

"It's good to be home." Tyler returned the greeting with the same friendly smile he had bestowed on Michael, then said in a more authoritative voice, "Will you please take our bags up to our rooms."

"Yes, sir." William became immediately mobile, moving toward the car and unloading the luggage.

"Your sister is in the living room, sir," Michael informed Tyler as he followed Tyler and Kate toward the house.

"I thought she was going to Europe for a month or more," Tyler said irritably, then at Kate's questioning glance, he added, "Claire is best taken in small doses or not at all. However, since she lives here too, you'll be running into her on occasion, and we may as well get the introductions over with."

Kate didn't like the way that sounded and would have suggested that, if meeting Claire was to be an ordeal, she would prefer to put it off for a while. But she was not given the opportunity.

Taking her by the elbow, Tyler led her through the marble-floored entrance hall and into a large living room decorated in the ornate French rococo style.

There was nothing homey about this room, Kate thought, feeling decidedly uncomfortable. Then, telling herself that if she had grown up in this house, she would feel differently, she was again acutely aware of the chasm between herself and Tyler.

"Welcome," said a petite and elegantly coiffured blond woman as she rose from a couch on the far side of the room. She was dressed in scarlet lounging pajamas, and as she spoke she gestured with an almost-empty crystal goblet.

"Isn't it a little early in the day for that?" Tyler asked with a scowl.

"It's only sherry," she returned haughtily, moving toward them with a slightly unsteady tread. "I make it a habit never to touch wine before noon and never any of the hard stuff until after five. Of course, an occasional glass of champagne with breakfast is always nice."

Grim disapproval registered on Tyler's face. "Kate, I would like you to meet my sister, Claire. Claire, this is Kate." The introductions were made with cool formality.

"It's so nice to finally meet you." Claire held out her free hand toward Kate in greeting.

"It's nice to meet you, too," Kate managed, forcing a smile. She reached out to accept Claire's hand only to have it withdrawn as soon as their fingers barely touched, as if Claire found the contact distasteful.

"It's so nice to have an experienced mechanic in the family," Claire said with an acid smile. "Doctors and lawyers are a dime a dozen but a truly excellent mechanic is a real treasure, I always say."

Tyler's eyes narrowed dangerously. "And I always say—" he began blackly only to be interrupted by Kate.

"Thank you so much." She returned Claire's smile with one of schooled innocence. "It's so nice to be considered a treasure by one's sister-in-law."

"Touché," Claire muttered, raising her glass in Kate's direction. Then frowning at its lack of contents, she moved away from them toward the liquor cabinet.

Tyler guided Kate out of the room and up the stairs, his expression black. "I want to apologize for my sister's behavior. Three bad marriages have left her somewhat bitter, and when she's intoxicated, she can be very rude."

Glancing over her shoulder toward the living room, Kate saw Claire standing just beyond the entrance watching them. Something about the intensity the woman was studying her with caused Kate to wonder if Claire was actually as inebriated as she appeared or if she merely used the pretense of intoxication to say things she didn't dare say sober. The thought had an unsettling effect.

Still, there was no sense in worrying about trouble before it came, especially when she had no control over the source, Kate decided resignedly, and made herself concentrate on the tour Tyler was giving her of their living quarters.

Entering the master bedroom, they found a spry gray-haired woman directing a maid who was unpacking their suitcases.

"Mr. Tyler, it's so good to have you home again." The woman stopped her instructions to approach Tyler and take his hand warmly in hers as she added with a warm smile, "And with a bride, at last."

"It's good to be home," he replied with equal warmth. Placing an arm around Kate's shoulders, he again made the necessary introductions, mentioning that Nancy Rider was not only the housekeeper at Langston Hall but Michael's wife.

"It's a pleasure to welcome you to your new home." The woman beamed at Kate, washing away the foul taste of Claire's hostile greeting.

As Kate responded to the woman, Tyler's gaze traveled back to the maid, who was continuing to unpack Kate's belongings. He stiffened and asked, "Isn't that my mother's furniture?"

"Yes," Nancy replied, glancing over her shoulder at the mahogany dresser and matching dressing table that held Tyler's attention. "Of all of the furniture we had stored in the attic, sir, those pieces looked as if they would fit in here the best. The wood was the same as what was already in here and the style is simple enough to blend in pleasantly." Then as her gaze swung back to Tyler, a worried look came into her eyes. "We did need something to put Mrs. Langston's clothes in, and I thought she would like to have a dressing table. However, if you would prefer to use other pieces, I will look again."

"No," Tyler said, his eyes still on the furniture. "Those will be fine."

Nancy continued to regard him worriedly, as if she was afraid she had done something very wrong, and Kate felt as if she had come in on the third act of a play and had missed the important portions of the plot.

Tyler abruptly broke the uncomfortable silence with, "We need to finish our tour, and I have some important phone calls to make before dinner." Then, taking Kate by the arm, he guided her out of the room and down the hall to the small room he had mentioned earlier as a possible private sitting room.

It was a corner room. Crossing over to the two curtained walls, Tyler drew back the draperies, revealing wide, floor-to-ceiling windows.

"It's charming," she breathed as sunlight streamed in, giving the room a cheerful atmosphere. Joining Tyler, she looked out at the formal rose garden in full bloom below.

"Then it's yours," he said. "I'll have Nancy arrange to have these boxes—" he gestured toward several cardboard boxes scattered over the floor "—removed and you may furnish it as you wish."

"Thank you," Kate responded gratefully, recalling Claire and seeing this room as a welcome sanctuary. Then continuing to gaze out the window, she added, "The rose garden is beautiful."

"Our mother was a rose lover," Claire's voice sounded from the doorway. "I don't remember her very well. I was only seven when she died. But Nancy never tires of telling me how Mother used to sit in the middle of that garden for hours on end."

The frown that had never quite left Tyler's face deepened once again. "Did you want something, Claire?"

"I forgot to mention the little dinner party I've arranged for this evening to introduce Kate to our friends," she replied with overly done innocence.

"A dinner party this evening?"

"A sort of after-the-fact wedding reception," Claire elaborated.

"You should have consulted me before making any plans," Tyler reprimanded her irritably. "Kate and I are tired. It would be better to put that sort of thing off for a couple of days."

"I could cancel," Claire said in honeyed tones. "But then our friends might think that Kate doesn't want to meet them or, even worse, that you're embarrassed to introduce her to them."

Tyler's gaze narrowed dangerously. "All right. Have your little party. Is it formal or informal?"

"Formal. I would offer Kate something to wear, but I'm afraid that nothing I own would fit her." A Cheshire cat grin belied the apology in Claire's voice.

"I'm sure I can find something suitable," Kate said, hating Claire's little games but not knowing how to stop them.

Nancy suddenly appeared behind Claire, her arms full of Kate's new clothing. "I'll have these lightly pressed before they're hung, Mrs. Langston," she said.

Claire's smile became a pout as she followed Nancy's retreating back with her eyes. "Tyler must have had every seamstress in New York working their little fingers to the bone all last week," she muttered sarcastically.

"I didn't want Kate's lack of the proper attire to cause her any grief," he said. "And now that you have informed us of your little party, why don't you go back downstairs.''

But Claire wasn't finished. As she swung back toward him, a gleam sparkled in her eyes. "I suppose this marriage means you'll give up that very cozy apartment in town, the one you use for those, ah, all-night business meetings and when you're too tired to drive back out here after an evening in the city."

"It has already been sublet for the duration of my lease," he replied, the tightening of his jaw indicating he was very close to losing his temper.

"Too bad." She sighed regretfully. "Life is going to be dull around here without Father storming through the house in the evenings demanding to know who you're bedding on any particular evening."

Kate felt her stomach twist, but outwardly she showed no reaction to Claire's obvious baiting, knowing that any reaction would only encourage the woman.

"Goodbye, Claire." This time Tyler's voice held a distinct threat.

Knowing it would be dangerous to remain, Claire rewarded him with a shrug and sauntered off down the hall.

"I'd better go make those phone calls," Tyler said into the sudden heavy silence.

"And I think that I should rest awhile if I'm to meet your friends tonight," Kate returned, with a calmness she didn't feel. She'd known that Tyler was experienced, but to have his experience thrown in her face was unnerving.

Returning to the bedroom, she lay down on the king-size bed and stared at the intricately carved design worked into the plaster ceiling. What she was feeling was jealousy, which made her furious with herself. She didn't want to care what Tyler had done or would do in the future when their arrangement was over.

Determinedly she forced herself to recall his anger that afternoon at the way he had been manipulated into their marriage. But even as the memory became vivid in her mind, she recalled how he had kissed her hand and made her feel as if it was the two of them together against the world.

"No!" she said aloud to herself. "He and I are only going to be a couple for a short time. After that we'll go our separate ways. There will be *no* enduring 'us against the world'!"

THE PARTY BEGAN EASILY ENOUGH. Kate had chosen a dusty-rose dress that complemented the gray of her eyes. Tyler commented on how lovely she looked, and when she entered the living room, she felt pretty and only a little nervous.

Several of the guests had already arrived. Tyler introduced her, and everyone was, at least on the surface, polite and friendly. She did notice a coolness in the eyes of a couple of the women, but the coolness did not extend to their greetings or conversation. Even Claire was well behaved.

One of the men was describing a trip he had recently taken to China, and Kate was actually beginning to relax when a sudden hush fell over the room.

Following everyone's line of vision, Kate saw a striking-looking woman standing at the entrance to the room. A couple of inches taller than Kate, she had burnished red hair and emerald-green eyes. The gown she wore was cut low, and the material draped gently along the lines of her body, showing off a figure that brought a low whistle from a couple of the men.

"Linda always could fill out a dress," a man standing next to Kate commented admiringly. Then, receiving a sharp glance from his female companion, he looked suddenly uncomfortable and became quiet.

"Tyler." The redhead smiled brightly and moved toward the group in which Tyler and Kate were standing.

Immediately the others in the cluster backed away a little, almost as if they sensed a skirmish coming and wanted to give the combatants room.

After kissing Tyler lightly on the cheek with a familiarity that caused Kate's toes to curl, the woman turned her full attention to Kate. "I'm Linda Mc-Greggor, an old friend of the family, and I want to wish you and Tyler the very best," she said in a low, throaty voice as she extended her hand in greeting.

Although Linda's manner was friendly, Kate didn't miss the ice in those green eyes as she accepted the handshake. She forced herself to ignore the feeling of impending battle and managed a level thank-you.

Linda's smile broadened while the ice in her eyes crystallized. "I hope you won't mind if I borrow Tyler once in a while for some business advice." Her gaze shifted to Tyler and the ice turned to fire. "My mother has finally decided to retire. That means I'll be taking over as chairman of the board at Chandra Cosmetics. I know I'll be running into difficulties occasionally that will require expert advice—so I hope you won't mind if I call on you to discuss various positions I might take."

"I could have sworn that Linda was already an expert in all of the positions," a woman behind Kate muttered. Kate tasted the bile that had risen to her throat and wondered if people could see evidence of the nausea she was feeling.

Then, surprising herself by her ability to appear in control, she slipped an arm through Tyler's, and with a smile at Linda, said coolly, "As long as you keep in mind that he's only available during business hours and in public places."

Linda's eyes glittered challengingly. "Public places are so stifling to intense business conver—"

"Kate!" Uriah's voice boomed from the doorway, rescuing her from a cattish fray she was not certain she could win and knew she was a fool to even enter. There was no doubt in her mind that Linda McGreggor was the Linda who had given Tyler the shaving kit and that as soon as their marriage was over, it would be back in Linda's bathroom.

Approaching Kate, Uriah said loudly and distinctly, "I'm so sorry I wasn't here to greet you when you arrived today. I'd been looking forward to your arrival, but I had an all-day business meeting that couldn't be avoided. It's so good to have you here at last." As he reached her, he gave her a giant bear hug to add even more emphasis to his words. Kate knew he was doing this to let everyone in the room know he thoroughly approved of his son's choice of a wife, but despite his obvious fondness for her, she couldn't help feeling like a piece of merchandise.

Uriah released her, and his gaze played briefly over Linda before he focused his attention on Tyler. "It's good to have you home, son," he said, shaking Tyler's hand. Then his voice took on a protective edge as he added, "I hope you've been taking good care of Kate."

"She's doing an adequate job of taking care of herself," Tyler responded dryly. Then in more conversational tones, he said, "Linda was just telling us she will be taking over as chairman of the board at Chandra Cosmetics. Perhaps you could give her a few pointers."

"I'd love to." Uriah beamed, turning to Linda as Tyler slipped an arm around Kate's waist and led her toward the other side of the room.

For Kate, the evening was ruined. She managed to present an amicable front, but she constantly found herself glancing at Linda.

By the time the evening was over and the last guest had finally left, she felt as if she'd spent hours walking a tightrope. She began to wish wholeheartedly that Uriah Langston had never set foot in Piperville.

Accompanying Tyler to their rooms, Kate promised herself to say nothing about the evening, but her mind and mouth refused to cooperate. "I assume Linda McGreggor is the Linda who would be happy to have you leave your shaving kit in her bathroom anytime," she heard herself saying as they entered the bedroom and Tyler closed the door.

"I have a new shaving kit," he replied, going over to the closet and taking out the kit he had used on their honeymoon.

He tossed it to her, and when she caught it, she stared at it for a moment before setting it aside. Again she told herself that she shouldn't care about Linda and Tyler's relationship, but she did. "The woman issued you a blatant invitation in front of everyone," she accused.

Tyler was watching her intently, his expression shuttered. "You actually sound jealous."

Pride stiffened Kate's back. "I realize that the woman has a great deal of appeal to the male of the species. I couldn't help noticing that a large portion of the men at the party tonight couldn't keep their eyes from wandering in her direction. Also, she is obviously wealthy in her own right and understands the business world on your level. I didn't realize how much your father had asked you to give up when he insisted upon our union. I'm sorry. He should never have made the demand and I would never have agreed if I'd known." Drawing a sharp breath, she finished, "I know we have an agreement, but I will not remain in this house while you're seeing Linda and the rest of the community is either calling me a fool or pitying me."

"I promised you fidelity for the duration of our marriage and you will have it," Tyler said, continuing to study her with interest.

"Now it's my turn to wonder if your mind is elsewhere when we are in bed together," she said, the thought knotting her stomach.

"I always know who I'm with." Crossing the distance between them, he caught her chin in his hand and looked hard into her face. "As for Linda being a loss for me, she is not. I admit we've been together on and off over the past few years, but there has never been anything serious between us. For a steady relationship, Linda prefers a man she can control. She turns to me when she gets bored."

"Apparently she's bored at the moment," Kate muttered acidly.

"People had her paired with me, and she doesn't like to look like a loser. She simply came to cause a little trouble. My marriage to you means absolutely nothing to her."

Kate's jaw tightened against the warmth of his touch as his hand continued to cradle her chin. "I find it very difficult to believe she wouldn't want you permanently if she could have you," Kate said, then wished she had remained silent as his gaze burned into her.

"A compliment from you is so rare that I find it unbelievably exciting," he said, tracing the line of her jaw with the tips of his fingers. "I think I might even enjoy flattery coming from you." His voice was a low growl as his breath played warmly against her skin. Drawing her into his embrace, he kissed the turned-down corners of her mouth.

Kate knew she was playing a fool's game but at the moment didn't care. She didn't want to think about Linda, about her red hair, flashing green eyes and flawless body. She wanted to be in Tyler's arms and, at least for a while, pretend he wanted to belong to her alone.

Meeting his lips with a hunger of her own, she ran her hands over his shoulders to the back of his neck, caressing the strong hard cords as her body melted invitingly against his.

"I've been wondering all evening if you're wearing one of those lacy next-to-nothings under that very sedate dress," he murmured as his mouth deserted hers to seek the sensitive hollow behind her ear.

Though he had periodically attempted to introduce lighthearted banter into their lovemaking, she had never entered the game. She had purposely held back, hoping to keep her feelings for her husband from intensifying in any way. Now she admitted helplessly that she couldn't stop them from growing stronger, and the desire to prove to him that she could be as sexy and exciting as any female he had known took control of her. "What makes you so certain I have anything on?" she asked huskily.

"Now that's a thought to set a man's imagination on fire," he growled, letting his hands play along the curves of her body, searching for evidence of what was or wasn't beneath the dress.

"You're tickling me," she giggled, wiggling seductively against him. The exhilaration she felt at his obvious arousal was unlike anything she'd ever experienced before.

"Tickling you wasn't what I had in mind." He nipped her neck, causing goose bumps to rise on her skin.

Having dropped all pretense of holding back, Kate was shocked by how much she wanted him. Slipping off his dinner jacket, she unfastened his tie and tossed it aside. Then, unfastening the top button of his shirt, she kissed the hollow of his neck. His flesh had an intoxicating flavor. Slowly she trailed kisses upward toward his mouth.

He accepted her lips fully, deepening the kiss until she trembled with desire. Then, breaking the contact with short gentle kisses, he lifted her away from him. "I think it's time I found out just what you do have on under this dress," he said gruffly.

She had chosen very conservative outer attire for this first meeting with his friends. Tiny rounded cloth-covered buttons held her dress closed from the choker-style collar to the hem. Removing the string of pearls from her neck, he laid them aside and applied himself to the long line of buttons. "This could take all night," he muttered as he finished with the first and moved to the second.

While she watched him with a quiet smile that belied the violent stirrings he created within her, she moved her hands, which had been resting at his waist, to his hips. "Not *all* night, I hope," she breathed huskily.

A hint of laughter added golden highlights to the dark brown of his eyes. "Not all night," he assured her, masculine approval entering his voice as he reached the ninth button and the thin piece of lace that was her bra began to show. "So you did wear one of those scanty sets from Paris."

"I didn't want you to be disappointed if the dinner turned out to be dull," she bantered, managing to keep her voice level even as the heat of his hands was setting her body on fire. She had wanted him before, but never with so frightening an intensity.

"Nothing, when you've been involved, has turned out to be dull." He smiled crookedly, kissing the hollow between her breasts before reapplying himself to the seemingly endless line of buttons.

Her breath locked in her lungs, and she swayed invitingly against him.

"You're not making this marathon unbuttoning session any easier," he growled in mock reproof, adding, "My hands are getting tired."

"That," she said, frowning in round-eyed, playful horror, "would be a disaster."

A low laugh issued from deep in his throat only to be drowned out by the sudden ringing of the phone.

"Damn!" Tyler glanced toward the instrument on the bedside table, which had buttons for several lines. "That has to be Hong Kong. The time difference is so great." For a moment he hesitated, then with a second muttered "Damn," he gave Kate a quick apologetic kiss, moved away and picked up the phone.

A heavy disappointment spread over her as she listened to the first few words of the conversation and realized this was going to be a long call. Walking over to the closet, she kicked off her shoes, then slipped off her panty hose.

She glanced back toward Tyler and noted that he was deep in a discussion. The mood was gone. Then her eyes fell on the shaving kit, and Linda's image came sharply into focus. Linda, she thought curtly, would never let a phone call interfere with her plans.

Purposefully walking over to where Tyler was sitting on the edge of the bed, she knelt in front of him and, taking her time, began to unfasten the buttons of his shirt, kissing each newly exposed area of flesh as she went. His breathing became ragged and she smiled, knowing that she could make him want her. When the shirt fell freely open, she brushed her cheek against his hair-roughened chest, luxuriating in its hot hard warmth. Her hands, resting on his thighs, felt his leg muscles tense, and currents of excitement flowed through her. She had never realized before how stimulating arousing a man could be.

"Hold on just a minute, Brian," Tyler said stiffly into the phone, then placing a hand over the mouthpiece, he frowned down at her. "You're making it very difficult for me to concentrate."

"That," she said mischievously, "was my intention."

"Kate . . ." he said warningly.

Her lips formed a pout as she breathed a resigned sigh and rose from her kneeling position in front of him. She didn't really want to disturb him if the call was important.

Standing a short distance away, she slowly finished unbuttoning her dress. As she slipped it off, she felt a prickling sensation and glanced at Tyler to find him watching her, his eyes dark with desire.

"Use your own judgment," he growled into the receiver, then dropped it into the cradle. Rising from the bed, he quickly crossed the distance between them.

She trembled from the heat of his touch as his hands moved possessively along the lines of her body, pausing to play with the small bits of lace underclothing before removing them. Then, drawing her down beside him on the bed, he growled, "Remind me never to take you to the office."

# CHAPTER SIX

KATE AWOKE THE NEXT MORNING to kisses being lightly feathered over her face.

"I wanted to say goodbye before I left for work," Tyler said gruffly as she slowly opened her eyes.

Still half asleep, she smiled and reached toward him, winding her arms around his neck. "Do you really have to go?"

"I'm afraid so." He frowned regretfully as he dropped a kiss on her lips before disentangling himself from her arms. "But I'll be home by six. In the meantime, I've instructed Nancy to have the boxes removed from the small room at the end of the hall and to have the windows and floor cleaned. You can decide if you want new draperies or the walls painted a different color. Then just tell Nancy and she'll see that your wishes are followed." Dropping another light kiss on her lips, he started for the door.

"Have a good day," she called out to his retreating back.

"You, too," he tossed over his shoulder as he disappeared into the hall, closing the door behind him.

The soft smile remained on Kate's face as she climbed out of the bed and dressed. She felt very close to Tyler and was beginning to believe that his feelings for her might be deepening.

Leaving the bedroom, she wandered down the hall to find that the boxes had already been removed from the room that was soon to be her private sanctuary. Two maids were inside, busily cleaning, and the Oriental carpet that had covered a major portion of the floor was rolled up in the hall. Kate unrolled a portion to look at the colors, which were ivory and pale blue. Glancing into the room, she noted that the walls were also ivory and the linen draperies came very close to matching the color of the walls, all of which gave the impression that the room was larger than it actually was. It also gave Kate a greater choice in furniture, and she decided to keep the draperies and walls as they were.

When she told Nancy of her decision, the woman smiled approvingly. "Melinda Langston, Tyler's mother," she said, "originally chose those colors. She felt they gave the room an open, cheery atmosphere, but also elegance. So much like her own personality." A sadness had entered the housekeeper's voice. Controlling herself, she said in a more professional manner, "It's been a long time since that room was used for anything other than storage. If it meets with your approval, I'll have the rug and draperies sent out for cleaning."

"That will be fine," Kate said, finding it a little difficult to get used to the idea of others taking the responsibility for seeing that work was done.

"I'll see to it today," Nancy said, nodding, then asked in a politely deferential voice, "Would you like to have breakfast on the patio so that you may enjoy the rose garden?"

"Yes," Kate agreed readily as her stomach began to growl, reminding her of the energy she had expended during the night. Her eyes sparkled at the memory.

"And when you're ready, I'll take you up to the attic and you can look over what furniture is available," Nancy offered.

"Thank you," Kate said. With others waiting on her hand and foot, she felt decidedly decadent—but enjoyed it immensely.

Out on the patio, a gentle breeze carried the fragrance of the roses to her, adding to the soothing, elegant atmosphere. As she ate her perfectly prepared breakfast, a joy she had rarely felt during her life filled her. To have all of this and Tyler, too, seemed like a dream. *It is,* the voice of reason stated bluntly, forcing her back to reality. *Tyler Langston does not love you!*

*But he could learn to,* she said to herself in rebuttal, recalling their lovemaking of the night before and the way he had awakened her with a kiss.

*He's just making the best of a situation that was forced on him,* the voice insisted.

Her joy tainted, Kate suddenly felt restless. She gulped the rest of her coffee and went in search of Nancy.

Entering the attic a few minutes later with the housekeeper, Kate was astonished at the amount and variety of furniture there.

"Most of this came from Nathaniel Langston's several wives," Nancy explained as she began lifting coverings so that Kate could see the pieces fully. "His portrait is hanging in the downstairs study. His first wife was a French countess he met on a trip abroad. At the time he brought her home, the house was furnished in Chippendale. She hated it. To please her, he had all the Chippendale stored and refurnished the house in Louis XV. Then she died in childbirth during the third year of their marriage. Next he married an English noblewoman who was appalled by the French decor but didn't like the Chippendale, either. Her taste ran to Victorian, and catering to her whims, Nathaniel allowed her to refurnish the house to suit herself. Shortly after the last piece was in place, she died of a fever. At that point, he swore he would marry only good solid pioneer stock and chose as his third wife the daughter of one of the local farmers. While she was happy to leave the furnishings basically Victorian, she collected bits and pieces of furniture from all over the world during her travels with Nathaniel. Then, of course, later generations of Langston wives added to the collection." A soft reminiscent smile played over the housekeeper's features. "Melinda Langston used to say that there wasn't a style of furniture ever created that hadn't been represented by at least one piece at one time or another in this attic.''

Unable to control her curiosity about Tyler's mother, Kate probed gently, ''She must have been very young when she died. I believe Tyler mentioned that his brother was only four at the time.''

''Yes.'' A deep sadness etched itself into Nancy's features. ''She was only thirty-eight. One minute she was full of life and the next she was gone. Such a tragic accident. It was a terrible shock to all of us. I never did trust horses.''

Kate frowned. ''Horses?''

''Mrs. Langston was an excellent horsewoman,'' Nancy elaborated. ''She loved to jump them. She was breaking in a new jumper when the horse balked. She was thrown and broke her neck. The doctor said that death was instantaneous. At least she didn't suffer. Mr. Uriah sold all the horses the next day and has never allowed another one on the place.''

''He must have loved her a great deal,'' Kate said, feeling a lump in her throat at the thought of the death of one so young and so loved.

''Everyone did,'' Nancy replied. Then, with a heavy sigh, she returned their conversation to the business at hand by asking, ''Do you have any particular tastes in furnishings?''

Kate would have liked to ask more questions, especially about Tyler, but sensing the woman's reluctance to continue along personal lines, she said, ''I've always loved Victorian love seats.''

"Over there." Nancy pointed, then headed toward a far corner of the attic, where she pulled the sheeting off a beautifully worked love seat.

A few minutes later, they had settled on the love seat, a Queen Anne tea table, a "lady's chair" and a "gentleman's chair," along with a small table to set between the two, and a small secretary desk with claw-and-ball feet.

"I'll have all of these pieces moved into the room as soon as it's cleaned," Nancy said, brushing the dust from her hands.

Again feeling decadent because others were doing all the work, Kate said apologetically, "I hope I'm not being a nuisance."

"No," Nancy assured her with a warm smile. "I'm very glad you're here. Through the years, I've worried about Mr. Tyler." Pausing for a moment, Nancy studied Kate's face, then continued in a quiet, somber voice. "I can still remember, as if it were yesterday, his shocked reaction to his mother's death. He was thirteen at the time—a very vulnerable, very impressionable age. He didn't cry when his father told him. He just stood staring at Mr. Uriah, as if it couldn't be true. All during the viewing and the funeral, he never shed a tear. After the graveside ceremony, the mourners came back to the house. After a while I noticed Tyler was missing and went looking for him. I found him in his mother's private sitting room. He was crying. When I entered, he stopped. I tried to explain to him that it was healthy to cry, but he got this fierce gleam in his eyes and told me he never wanted to feel that way again. He said he would never care for another person as deeply as he had cared for his mother. At the time I thought this was just a cry of despair and he would outgrow it. But afterward he never did become attached to anyone very strongly. Even his feelings toward his father seemed to become cooler, as if he was building a wall around his emotions. I hated to think of him growing into a cold hard man.... But you've changed that. You've taught him how to love again." Taking Kate's hand, Nancy held it warmly for a long moment. "You could never be a nuisance as far as I'm concerned."

"Thank you," Kate managed, as all hopes of Tyler ever learning to love her vanished. The voice of reason had been right. He was simply making the best of a situation he'd been forced into.

She returned to the suite of rooms she shared with Tyler and entered the billiard room. After setting up the balls, she hit the cue ball with a force that sent the racked balls spinning wildly across the table. "Fates," she muttered grimly.

"Don't tell me you even know how to play pool," Claire said from the doorway. She breathed an exaggerated sigh and, as she entered, added in acid tones, "My father already thinks you're perfect. He thinks I should get to know you better...that you might be able to 'improve' me."

"I don't play a very good game of pool and I'm not perfect, nor do I make a habit of trying to improve other people," Kate replied tightly, wanting to tell the woman to get out but still too uncertain of her own place in the household to behave that rudely.

"Mind if I play?" Claire asked. The question was obviously meant to be strictly rhetorical, since she was already crossing the room to take a cue from the rack on the wall. "We'll make it straight pool. You broke and didn't send any balls into the pockets, so it's my turn."

With a shrug, Kate took a step back from the table and watched the small blonde line up her shot.

"The three ball in the corner pocket," Claire announced, sending the cue ball to its mark perfectly. Straightening, she walked slowly around the table to determine the next line of attack. She paused when she came to a spot directly opposite Kate and regarded her adversary musingly. "I have to admit that I'm very surprised by my brother's choice for a bride."

"No more than I was," Kate answered with dry honesty.

A tiny smile played at the corners of Claire's mouth. "Seven ball in the side pocket," she said, and again, with the expertise of a veteran, made the cue ball obey her command. Then, straightening, she looked at Kate. "My brother's entire life has been devoted to his work. I always expected that, if he married, it would be to further that interest—like the kings who used to marry to secure their borders or increase their holdings or both. I expected Tyler's choice either to be very wealthy in her own right or to have a controlling interest in a company he was interested in." A malicious challenge glittered in Claire's eyes. "Do you have any hidden assets, Kate?"

"No," Kate managed levelly as bile rose from her stomach. Claire knew her brother well.

Again a smile played over Claire's face as she returned her attention to the pool table. "Six ball in the corner pocket," she stated, sinking the ball with ease. She straightened and regarded Kate with a studious frown. "It's hard to imagine my brother in love. I've never honestly believed he knew the meaning of the word. He's always had a certain coolness about him, and his views on marriage have been cynical, to say the least."

Kate felt as if she was being stalked, and her back stiffened. She'd had enough of Claire's baiting. "Maybe," she suggested cuttingly, "he was simply reacting to some of the marriages he saw around him."

"Seven ball in the corner pocket," Claire snarled, hitting the cue ball with too much force and missing her shot. This time her eyes were ice as she faced Kate. "My father was the reason for my marriages falling apart. He was constantly threatening to disown me and accusing me of making irresponsible choices. He's very big on responsibility." Malice glittered in the dark depths of Claire's eyes. "He seems to think you're a walking paragon of responsibility. Tell me, Kate, what is the first step I should take toward behaving responsibly?"

"You could start by accepting the responsibility for your own mistakes," Kate replied coolly.

Dropping her cue onto the felt, Claire braced her hands on the table edge and leaned toward Kate. "My father," she said with biting sarcasm, "bought off my third husband behind my back."

"A man who can be bought off isn't worth having," Kate returned.

"And what about a wife?" Claire threw back, a challenge glittering in her eyes. For a long moment she watched Kate in cold silence, then walked with haughty dignity from the room.

As she stared at the closed door, Kate felt ill. She wondered if Claire knew the truth behind her marriage to Tyler. No one was supposed to know. Even Uriah didn't have all of the facts.

*She's just guessing,* Kate's voice of reason assured her. *You were poor and you married rich. There are a lot of people who'll believe you did it for the money.*

And when it came right down to the bottom line, she had! Kate reminded herself curtly. That was why Claire's parting shot had stung so badly. It had hit its mark.

A self-derisive cynicism etched itself into Kate's features. In one morning she had been given two different reasons why Tyler did not and would never love her. First, there had to be respect before there could be real love, and he couldn't possibly respect a woman he had bought. Second, he didn't want to fall in love, and she had never known a stronger-willed man.

Briefly she considered leaving and eventually paying him back all of the money he had spent on her and her family. But that would mean he would not gain control of Langston Industries, and she couldn't do that to him. Like it or not, she cared.

The walls felt as if they were closing in on her. She had to get away from this house and think. After a quick stop to pick up her purse, she went downstairs to find Nancy. She told the housekeeper that she would like to go sightseeing in Salem.

Within five minutes, William was pulling up in front of the house in a long black limousine.

During the drive, Kate sat in the cavernous passenger section and tried to sort out her situation. How could she have been so stupid as to allow herself to fall in love with Tyler Langston?

It wasn't by choice, she defended herself.

Maybe it was only infatuation, a hopeful voice of reason suggested. He could be very charming when he wanted to be, and he was an experienced, exciting lover.

Infatuation! She clung to this possibility like a drowning person who had just been tossed a life preserver. If it was infatuation, it would fade with time.

"Shall I drive you by the house that people say was the setting for Hawthorne's *The House of the Seven Gables*?" William asked over the intercom, breaking into Kate's thoughts.

"Yes, please, do," she answered.

But the house that had captured Hawthorne's imagination didn't hold Kate's interest any more than the rest of the sights in Salem.

Even on her walking tour, with the loud chatter of tourists filling the air, she couldn't get Tyler out of her mind. She pictured him as a grieving boy and then saw him more clearly as the man she knew—the man whose only goal in life was to have control of Langston Industries.

But he wasn't a user. He did show concern for others. He was taking very good care of her mother and brother and sister, as well as herself.

Only because he needed her cooperation, her cynical side insisted on pointing out. His father would probably declare the deal invalid if he learned the truth behind Tyler's arrangement with her.

Exhausted by the emotional battle she was waging to keep her relationship with Tyler in the proper perspective and feeling no more relaxed or less confused, Kate returned to Langston Hall.

Tyler greeted her with a frown. "I was beginning to worry," he said, coming out of his study as she reached the top of the stairs.

"Is it that late?" Glancing at her watch, she saw that it was already half-past six. Her expression became apologetic. "We got caught in traffic."

"Nancy said you went into Salem to do some sightseeing," he said conversationally as he accompanied her down the hall and opened the bedroom door.

"I'm not used to sitting around doing nothing, so I thought I'd put some of my newly found freedom from the daily grind to use by broadening my historical education," she tossed back with schooled levity. Then as her earlier encounter with Claire flashed vividly through her mind, she added, "And I was in the mood to see where they used to burn witches."

Dropping her purse on a chair, she turned to find Tyler regarding her coolly.

"We were expected downstairs ten minutes ago for drinks," he said in irritation. "I'll be in my study when you're ready."

He was angry. She frowned as she watched him leave, closing the door sharply behind him.

"Being a little late is no crime," she muttered defensively as she flicked a brush through her hair before adding fresh lipstick. "Besides, he knew where I was and I'm not used to punching a time clock."

Then her frown turned into an expression of concern. He had told her he would be home at six. He had probably had a very rough day, and her not being there when he arrived had only added another worry to what was already a long list of irritations.

Suddenly pausing in midmotion, she stared at the image in the mirror. Instead of thinking of him as being too unbending and demanding, annoyed simply because she had not been home to greet him, she was making excuses for his anger.

The frown returned to her face as her hope that what she was feeling for the man was merely infatuation dimmed.

# CHAPTER SEVEN

THE NEXT MORNING Kate awakened in time to have breakfast with Tyler and Uriah.

"I'm taking Father with me into work today," Tyler informed her as he finished his second cup of coffee and prepared to leave the table. "The Rolls he usually goes in isn't running properly, so William will be working on it today. If you want to do any more sightseeing, you may use the Cadillac, or if you prefer a smaller car, the BMW." As he spoke, he handed her a gold key ring with sets of keys to both cars dangling from it. "There are maps in the glove compartments. Try to keep in mind that you are not driving in the Indianapolis 500."

"Thank you, I will," she said, receiving his perfunctory kiss on the cheek with a plastic smile. In spite of his mild attempt at humor, she sensed anger beneath his polite facade. He had been withdrawn the evening before, and because of bits of conversation between Tyler and Uriah that she'd heard, she wondered if there was trouble at the Texas office. Tyler might have been worried about having to go there and bail Ross out. Watching him leave, she hoped that if he did have to go, he would take her with him. The thought of remaining in the house without him unnerved her. As much as she tried, she did not feel at home.

*That's because you aren't,* her voice of reason pointed out as she picked up the keys and carried them upstairs. *You are simply a temporary occupant.*

The thought didn't help her restlessness. In fact, it served to increase it. Wandering down the hall to her future sitting room, she found a maid busily cleaning the upholstery on the chairs and sofa she had chosen the day before.

"Mrs. Rider likes to have everything spotless," the maid explained, pausing to wipe a wayward strand of hair from her face.

Kate forced a smile and backed out of the room. No sanctuary there, she thought grudgingly as she went downstairs and out into the rose garden. But as pretty as it was, she wasn't the type to spend her days loitering in a garden. Besides, there was the possibility that Claire might decide to join her for another little chat.

Without really thinking about where she was going, she found herself nearing the garage. A silver-and-gray Rolls with the hood up was parked in the wide driveway, and interest sparked within her. Toby had said she was a natural mechanic, and she had enjoyed working on cars. Besides, a Rolls wasn't just any car; it was special. The urge to look under the hood was too strong to deny.

William had spread a blanket over the fenders on each side of the hood to protect the finish from his tools and the grease. As she approached, he looked up from the manual he'd been frowning at and schooled his expression into one of polite servitude. "Is there something I can do for you, Mrs. Langston?"

"No," Kate replied with an equally polite smile. Then in mildly hesitant tones, she said, "Actually, if you don't mind, I would like to take a look under the hood. I've done some mechanic's work but I've never seen a Rolls engine."

"Be my guest," he invited, watching slightly dubiously.

"I know I've never seen a cleaner engine," she said as she looked with fascination at what was considered one of the best made cars in the world. "It's beautiful."

"But it doesn't sound beautiful." William's frown returned. "I can't seem to locate the problem."

"May I look at the manual?" Kate asked, her gaze traveling to the book he had laid aside.

At his nod, she walked around to his side of the car, picked up the book and began leafing through it. "I would really like to help," she said. "I could follow you step by step through the manual. That way you won't overlook anything. Usually when the problem is hard to find, it's because it's something so small you don't even think about it. At least that's been my experience."

William regarded her dubiously, obviously uncertain of how to handle the situation. "I can't impose on you, Mrs. Langston," he said with stiff politeness.

"It's not an imposition." Kate knew she was forcing herself on the man, but she also knew that doing nothing was driving her slowly crazy, and she honestly did want to work on the car. "Working on a Rolls would be an honor," she said, and before he could refuse her offer again, she asked, "Do you have an extra pair of coveralls?"

"In the metal wardrobe over there," he replied, nodding toward a far corner of the garage.

"Thanks," she said, and within five minutes she was dressed and reading from the manual as William reinspected the engine step-by-step.

At first he continued to react politely but uncomfortably to her presence, but after a short while her genuine interest in the mechanics of the car created a mutual bond and they both relaxed.

They were concentrating so intently on their work that they didn't notice the passing of time or when Nancy approached with William's lunch.

"Mrs. Langston," the housekeeper addressed Kate with a look of surprise, "I thought that you had gone out sightseeing again."

Straightening from her bent-over position under the hood, Kate met the woman's mildly shocked expression with a smile. "William has been allowing me to help him with the Rolls."

"He really shouldn't have imposed." Nancy's gaze traveled from her son to Kate, a worried expression building in her eyes.

"Actually, I'm the one who imposed on him," Kate said hurriedly. "I'm not used to spending my time idly, and I love working on cars. The fact is that his allowing me to help saved me from an acute attack of boredom."

"I'll set you a place at the table for lunch," Nancy said, still regarding Kate uncertainly.

Kate stopped her. "No, please," she said. "Would you just bring me a sandwich out here? We're barely halfway through, and I'm having too much fun to let William continue alone."

For a moment Nancy looked as if she was going to object. Obviously she didn't feel that one of the ladies of the house should be working under the hood of a car. However, being a well-trained servant, she simply said, "Of course, Mrs. Langston."

"I'm afraid your mother doesn't approve of me at the moment," Kate said as she watched the housekeeper's retreating back.

"She likes you," William assured her. "But she's of the old school and believes that servants and their employers each have their own place and never the twain shall mingle."

"I had the impression you felt the same," Kate said, "and I want to apologize for imposing on you."

"I don't mind." William rewarded her with a warm smile. "You really are a good mechanic, and I'm not impressed with class differences. However, I do believe in not ruffling any feathers. I want to have my own car-repair shop someday and specialize in fixing imports like this Rolls. Of course, I want the Langstons' blessings and referrals of their friends."

"To your success," declared Kate, toasting him by raising a wrench as if it were a glass. Then with a relaxed smile, she returned her attention to the manual.

It was late in the afternoon when William finally announced he thought they had solved the problem. He offered Kate the privilege of turning on the engine for the final test.

Wiping the grease from her hands—the result of her inability to control the urge to do some actual work—she slid behind the wheel and switched on the ignition. The Rolls purred.

"Nice work, Mrs. Langston," William said as she turned the car off and joined him for a final look under the hood.

"It was my pleasure," she assured him.

The sound of a car coming up the drive caught her attention. Turning around, she saw it was Tyler's silver Porsche.

He parked in the garage and walked toward them, his expression shuttered. "May I assume from the smiles on your faces that the Rolls is fixed?" he asked, his cold gaze traveling from William to Kate.

"Yes, sir." William was immediately the proper servant, his smile replaced by a respectful expression. "Shall I drive into town and pick up Mr. Uriah?"

"I brought him home. I dropped him off at the front door before driving around to the garage," Tyler said, his attention never leaving Kate. An edge of reprimand entered his voice as he added, "You have a grease smear on your cheek. Perhaps you should consider returning to the house now in order to give yourself time to clean up and dress for dinner."

Furious at being spoken to as if she were a child caught playing hooky, but not wanting to create a scene, she set her mouth in a tight, straight line as she met Tyler's cool gaze with a matching frostiness. "I was just on my way."

"I apologize, Mr. Tyler," William said in formal tones. "I shouldn't have taken up Mrs. Langston's time with my work."

Kate turned to face William. She had forced him to accept her help, and she refused to allow him to also accept the brunt of Tyler's foul mood. "You didn't ask for my help—I insisted. I want to thank you for the privilege of working on the Rolls." Then before any more could be said, she stalked to the corner of the garage to remove the coveralls.

"Mrs. Langston is a very good mechanic, sir," William said, obviously attempting to soothe the situation as the two men watched Kate slip out of the coveralls and rehang them in the metal wardrobe.

"She's very good at a great many things," Tyler muttered grimly under his breath.

Returning to the men, Kate ignored Tyler. She smiled warmly at William and said, "Good evening, William," and then, without pausing, continued toward the house. Her anger was building by the second and, a few moments later, when Tyler fell into step beside her, she glanced toward him hostilely. "You embarrassed me in front of William," she hissed. "I am not a child and I will not be treated like one—especially like one who has misbehaved."

"No, you are not a child," he acknowledged darkly. "And therefore you should have known better than to have behaved the way you did today. You embarrassed Nancy and Michael. Michael came out to apologize to me when I stopped to let my father out at the house."

"I embarrassed them?" she demanded in shocked disbelief.

"William is their son," Tyler explained, his tone again like that of an adult speaking to a difficult child. "You, whom they see as one day becoming the mistress of Langston Hall, spent the day doing his work for him."

"If he was the gardener, no one would have objected," she argued. "I've seen pictures of women who are considered the very cream of society working in their gardens."

"You've seen them cutting a few flowers," Tyler corrected. "And gardens cannot be compared to working on car engines with the chauffeur."

"Then I apologize for not living up to the Langston name," Kate snapped, adding with barely contained fury, "I'm just not used to living in a class-oriented society." Then picking up her pace, she preceded him into the house.

"Well, well, if it isn't our female mechanic home from a hard day at the garage," Claire said, her drink raised in a mock toast. "I would have gone over to see what interesting things you were doing, but you and William looked as if you were having such a good time together I didn't want to disturb you."

Kate was tempted to make a response, but feeling Tyler's cold glare on the back of her neck, she chose instead to ignore Claire and continue up the stairs.

Passing through the bedroom without pausing, she entered the bathroom and quickly discarded her clothes. She stepped into the shower and hoped the hot water cascading over her would help wash away her anger, but to no avail. Tyler had humiliated her, treated her like a child over whom he expected to have complete control. Even if he was having business troubles because of his brother, he had no right to take his frustrations out on her.

Leaving the bathroom a little while later with a towel wrapped around her hair and another around her body, her cheeks still flushed with indignant anger, she found Tyler pacing the bedroom.

His anger was also clearly evident as he captured her by the upper arms and pinned her in front of him. "I want you to stay away from William," he ordered curtly. "I realize you have a penchant for mechanics, but my father will not tolerate your having an affair or even an innocent flirtation." His hands tightened painfully. "I expect you to live up to our agreement and that includes fidelity."

As she stared at him in stunned silence, he released her abruptly and slammed out of the room. For a long moment, she continued to stand in shocked silence, staring at the closed door in disbelief. Then, hearing his study door open and close, she suddenly became mobile. She forgot she was clothed in nothing more than a couple of towels and stormed across the hall.

He was punching in a number on the phone when her finger came down on the button, breaking the connection. "I resent the implication of what you just said," she said, seething.

Meeting the fury in her eyes, he said cuttingly, "They didn't burn witches in Salem."

"What?" she demanded, too angry to think and totally thrown off guard by his statement.

"They didn't burn witches in Salem," he repeated in icy tones. "They hanged a few, but they never burned any of them."

Kate continued to stare at him in angry confusion. "I don't understand what that has to do with your implication that I might be flirting with William."

"Why don't you tell me where you were yesterday and then we will discuss what you might or might not be up to," he suggested sarcastically.

Her jaw hardened. "I was in Salem."

"If you were in Salem sightseeing as you said," Tyler countered grimly, "then you would know that no witches were actually burned."

The knuckles of her hands whitened as she gripped the towel she was holding in place more tightly. "I wandered around the town, but I didn't see much of anything. I was too absorbed in my own thoughts. I was trying to determine what my place is here in Langston Hall." A sharpness entered her voice as she added, "The home of the aristocratic Langstons."

"You are my wife," he growled. "That is your place here, and I expect you to act the part even if you don't like it."

Kate's jaw tightened defensively. "I cannot sit idly around Langston Hall for two years, and I cannot fit into the type of life Claire leads. I don't play bridge, and I've never learned how to balance a tea cup in one hand and one of those little dessert dishes in the other and at the same time chew and spit out anyone who isn't present. I'm used to taking care of myself and having others depend on me."

"You *are* taking care of yourself and you do have others depending on you," he pointed out. "At the present time, your behavior determines not only your own well-being, but that of your mother and brother and sister."

The blatant reminder that her cooperation was being bought caused her stomach to churn. "I did not sell myself to you willingly," she reminded him fiercely as hot tears, held captive by pride, burned behind her eyes. "I had no acceptable alternative, and I'll go crazy if I have to sit around this house for two years with nothing constructive to occupy my time. I have to have something to do and I enjoy working on cars. That was why I was at the garage today, and that was the only reason!" Then because she was afraid she might lose control and refused to let him see her cry, she stalked out of the study and back into the bedroom.

The room felt cold and she began to shiver. Hot tears began to roll down her cheeks. So many arrows were piercing her armor that she wasn't certain which was the cause of her misery. Tyler had accused her of flirting with another man. He had even indicated that he felt she was capable of having an affair almost immediately after meeting a man. Then there was his harsh reminder that he considered her bought and fully paid for.

Well, she wasn't! Stalking over to the closet, she pulled out a pair of her old jeans and a shirt. She would leave with what she had owned before Tyler Langston had come into her life. He could keep his fancy wardrobe and his jewels, and she would pay back every cent he had spent on her family even if it took her the rest of her life.

Discarding the towels, she pulled on the jeans and then the shirt.

"While you do fill out a pair of jeans nicely," Tyler said as he entered and closed the door behind him, "they are not proper attire for my father's dinner table."

"That is because I have no intention of sitting at your father's dinner table," she informed him curtly, finishing buttoning her shirt and beginning to pull the rest of her clothes off the hangers to toss them onto a nearby chair.

Crossing the room in long angry strides, Tyler caught her by the arm and turned her toward him. "We have a deal, Kate, and it's too late for you to back out."

"I'm not a piece of property you own, Tyler Langston," she snarled, attempting to pull free only to have his grip tighten.

"I don't think of you as being owned," he growled, his jaw set in a hard, determined line. "I think of you as being a partner in a business deal in which we both stand to gain or lose a great deal, and I expect you to live up to your part of it."

He was right. She had agreed to his bargain, and she did believe him when he said he did not think of her as something he owned. But her anger and hurt were still strong. She faced him icily and stated, "I am not a wanton woman."

Releasing her, he raked a hand through his hair as a self-derisive smile curled one corner of his mouth. "I know," he admitted. Then his eyes darkened, but not with anger. His gaze traveled down her figure and then back up as he said, "But you are a damned sexy one, especially when you're not wearing any underthings."

A flush built from her neck upward. "I was too angry to look for any."

"I'll have to remember not to make you angry just before we dress to go out," he mused dryly, "or you could start a riot."

He began to unfasten the buttons of her shirt, and her body trembled with the desire he could so easily spark. Horrified that, as angry as he had made her, she could still be made to want him so easily, she stiffened and started to step away.

Annoyance flickered behind the dark desire in his eyes, and his hands slid under her shirt to burn their imprint into her flesh as he held her possessively in front of him. "Your presence in my bed is one of the privileges I have according to our agreement," he growled huskily, "and I have no intention of being deprived of it."

Standing frozen in front of him, she allowed him to finish unbuttoning her shirt and remove it. His touch sent currents of electricity through her, warming and stimulating the woman inside, bringing back sharp memories of how exciting being possessed by him could be. It took every ounce of her strength to remain stoic and immobile, but she was determined to show no reaction. She hated his feeling that he had a right to claim her body whenever he wanted it. But even more, she hated her treacherous body for wanting him to claim her.

"Don't look as if you're attending a funeral," he chided, his anger becoming more visible. "Or do you plan to lie to me and tell me you've never enjoyed our lovemaking?"

Moistening her lips, she said tightly, "No, I just never thought of it as *your right*."

The anger in his eyes lessened as his hands traveled caressingly along the line of her shoulders and down her arms. "I did not say it was my *right*," he corrected her gruffly. "I said it was my *privilege*." His hands left her arms and traveled upward over her rib cage until they cradled her breasts.

Her body flamed with such intense desire that she wasn't sure how long her legs would hold her upright. His thumb teased a hardening nipple as his lips brushed hers. "Having you in my bed has been one of the most gratifying experiences of my life."

The sincerity in his voice seriously weakened her resistance. As he unfastened the snap of her jeans and pulled down the zipper to allow himself free access to the roundness of her hips, it crumbled entirely.

"I want you, Kate," he growled, drawing her firmly against him to prove the strength of his need.

A soft moan broke from her lips as all pretense of not wanting him as badly as he wanted her vanished.

A slow smile played over his features. "Your eyes have the strangest white highlights when you are in a wanting mood," he said huskily, and picking her up, he carried her to the bed.

THE SUN STREAMING through the windows of her now completed sitting room could not brighten Kate's spirit the next morning as she paced the tiny room. Tyler had won again!

She was still in the Langston household living up to her part of the agreement, and her activities were still restricted.

"I may become a leading expert on sights to see in and around Boston," she mused grimly, pausing to stare down at the rose garden below and wishing she could interest herself in gardening.

"Of course, there's always volunteer work." She frowned. The thought wasn't exciting, but such work would help pass the time.

A knock on the door interrupted her frustrated contemplations.

"A man is here with, uh, something for you," Nancy announced dubiously when Kate answered the welcome interruption.

"What kind of a something?" Kate asked, Nancy's hesitance making her uneasy.

"I believe it's supposed to be a gift," the housekeeper replied, adding apologetically, "I thought perhaps it was a mistake, but the man insists it's for Kate Langston and says you must sign for it personally." A pleading quality entered Nancy's voice. "I'm afraid he means to remain parked in front of the house until you come down."

Kate followed Nancy down the stairs and out the front door. A young man wearing grease-smeared coveralls and carrying a clipboard cowered against a tow truck while Claire, looking somewhat wild in a brilliant blue kimono brightly decorated with embroidered peacock feathers, glared at him hostilely.

"What...?" Kate began, only to swallow the question as her eyes traveled past the truck to the flatbed trailer it pulled. On the trailer sat what had once been a very expensive sports car. Now its paint, or what was left of it, was an indistinguishable color, the tires were bald and the leather upholstery was torn, its stuffing half in, half out. Adding a slash of incongruency was a bright red ribbon wrapped around the hood and tied in an enormous bow.

"Kate Langston?" the young man said hopefully, keeping a cautious eye on Claire as if he half expected her to physically attack him at any moment.

"Yes," Kate said, nodding, a slow smile beginning to form on her face.

"If you'll just sign here—" the young man extended the clipboard in Kate's direction "—and tell me where you want it placed..."

But Kate's attention was riveted on the car. "What make is it?" she asked.

"It's a Jaguar XK120, ma'am."

"It doesn't look like any Jaguar I've ever seen," Claire said, scowling.

"It's a vintage year," the young man informed her, as if he thought she must be blind not to have seen the beauty beyond the rust and destruction.

"It's a piece of junk!" Claire snapped back, shooting him a glare that brought a hint of fear into his eyes. Turning her attention to Kate, she said sternly, "Don't you dare sign for it until you find out who sent it."

Nancy, who had been watching in silence, suddenly spoke up. "Miss Claire is right," she said reasonably. "It would be prudent to find out who would send you such . . . an unusual gift before you accept it."

"There's a note attached to the steering wheel," the young man pointed out hastily, obviously anxious to make his delivery and escape the peacock-clad woman's threatening gaze.

Kate was fairly certain she knew who had sent the car, and a happy excitement filled her as she climbed onto the flatbed trailer and untied the note from the steering wheel. She opened it, and her eyes glittered as she read:

Dear Kate,

Being married to you is a genuinely unique experience. No other man I know has a wife who would want a car in this condition. However, you are a challenge, and since one challenge deserves another, I thought this gift might appeal to you.

William knows where to buy the parts you might need and where to have this "vintage car," as it was referred to, painted and reupholstered when the time comes.

Have all the bills sent to me, since the costs are meant to be part of the gift. Have fun.

—Tyler

He did understand! Tears glistened in her eyes.
"Well?" Claire demanded.

"It's from Tyler," Kate replied, picking up the dozen long-stemmed red roses lying in the driver's seat and climbing down from the flatbed trailer.

Claire's eyes rounded in shock. "I'm beginning to think we may have to have my brother committed. And I always thought of him as such a sane man." Shaking her head as if she found the whole situation intolerable, she went back into the house.

Ignoring her sister-in-law, Kate handed the flowers to Nancy. "Would you please put these in some water and place them in my sitting room while I go with the driver and show him where to leave the car."

"Yes, ma'am," Nancy replied, still regarding the situation dubiously. "If you say so, Mrs. Langston." Then, accepting the flowers, she followed Claire inside.

"The car is not in as bad a shape as it looks," the young man assured Kate as she signed the receipt. "It just needs a little work."

"A lot of work," she corrected, climbing into the tow truck beside him.

"A lot of work," he admitted.

As they neared the garage, they found William waiting. "Mr. Langston called and told me to clear a space near the workbench," he said, regarding the Jaguar as doubtfully as his mother had.

"Good," Kate said happily, climbing out of the tow truck and standing aside to allow the two men to move the Jaguar into the garage.

"Mr. Langston said that the car needed a lot of work," William commented as the tow truck drove away and he walked slowly around the vintage automobile. "But I would say that was an understatement."

"But it'll keep me busy," Kate returned delightedly, more to herself than to William.

"That it will," he agreed.

Returning to the house, she changed into an old pair of jeans and a sweatshirt. Then, covering her hair with a bandanna, she started back to the garage.

Nancy met her at the foot of the stairs. "Your flowers are in your sitting room," she said, then added hesitantly, "And Miss Claire is in her room with a headache. She asked me to ask you if your . . . gift was out of sight of the neighbors."

"Any neighbor who can see over a ten-foot-high wall and through the woods at the side and back of the garage wouldn't be stopped by any camouflage I could design," Kate replied with a mischievous gleam in her eyes, too happy to let Claire's attitude bother her. "However, if the question is, can any of her friends see it if they come to call, then the answer is no. It's inside the garage on the far end next to the BMW."

"Thank you. I'll tell her, Mrs. Langston," Nancy said. Then, as if she needed to convince herself that everything was all right, she added as she continued down the hall, "I do suppose that Mr. Langston knows what he's doing."

*Tyler Langston always knows what he's doing,*
Kate's inner voice said, as if to dampen her excitement and keep her perspective clear.

Still, a glitter of joy remained in her eyes as she
walked toward the garage. She didn't care if Tyler was
using the car to pacify her. It wasn't something he had
to do. They had an agreement, and she had promised
to live up to it.

*Just don't let this display of understanding lead you
to expect something more,* her inner voice warned.

"I won't," she murmured aloud, the glitter fading.
"I won't."

# CHAPTER EIGHT

FOUR MONTHS LATER Kate stood in nearly the same spot in which she had first seen the Jaguar. This time, however, no one would describe the car in front of her as a piece of junk. The now fully operable vintage car had just been returned from the body shop with new kid-leather upholstery in a soft doe brown and its exterior painted white and polished to a high luster.

Her masterpiece was finished. Smiling to herself, she recalled that it was Claire who had caused the family to begin referring to the Jaguar in artistic terms.

"Tyler, I'm beginning to think you may need psychiatric care," she had announced as they'd sat down to dinner the evening of the car's arrival. "I absolutely refuse to admit to my friends that my brother gave his wife a wreck as a gift and, even worse, that she was thrilled. It could set off a trend that would lead to several divorces. I have given this situation a great deal of thought all afternoon and have concluded I will tell everyone that Kate has decided to interest herself in avant-garde art and the Jaguar is a project she is considering as a fountain piece for the rose garden."

"It might be interesting to be considered an artist," Kate had mused. "I could trade my scarves in for berets, and if I don't feel like being sociable, people will simply explain my reclusive behavior by saying it's part of my artistic temperament."

"I was under the impression that women didn't feel they required any excuses for their moods," Tyler had said dryly. "I thought it was all part of the feminine mystique."

While Claire had regarded her brother irritably, Kate had shaken her head in mock dismay. "And just when I was about to stop thinking of you as an incurable chauvinist," she had said with exaggerated exasperation.

"It's always unwise to give a man the benefit of the doubt," Claire had cautioned cynically.

Tossing his daughter an "I'm not interested in hearing your views on men" glance, Uriah had raised his glass toward Kate. "I propose a toast to the artistic temperament. May it serve Kate well."

And from that moment on, the idea that Kate was an aspiring sculptor had become an inside family joke.

Lovingly caressing the curve of the fender, Kate was a little sorry that the car was finished. Many happy memories connected it with Tyler.

A smile played across her face as she recalled the laughter in his eyes when he had arrived home from work the night of the car's arrival and she had thanked him profusely. "Keeping you happy, Kate," he'd said, "is proving to be a very unique undertaking."

And then there had been the interest he had taken in her project. She'd expected him to ignore her activities once he was satisfied her time was being occupied in a way that kept her appeased.

But one morning about a week after the car's arrival, he had climbed out of bed and tossed her jeans and shirt onto her blanket-covered body. "Time to get up, my lady mechanic," he'd ordered. "I want to see what you've been up to." Then he, too, had dressed in jeans and a pullover and, after breakfast, accompanied her to the garage, where he'd proceeded to spend the entire morning asking questions and helping out. After that, to her surprise, there had been several other instances when he had taken time out of his busy schedule to work with her in the garage.

But the one memory that was the most vivid and meant the most to her was of the day she had seriously considered giving up on the car. A few times, the repair work had not gone as smoothly as she'd hoped. But on this particular occasion she'd become so frustrated that she was honestly considering throwing in the wrench and conceding victory to the car.

Tyler arrived home from work that day to find her in her sitting room, scrubbed and dressed for one of Claire's cocktail parties.

"Don't look so miserable," he said, tilting her face upward to place a light kiss on her forehead. "I'll take you out to dinner and a movie. That way we'll both escape a boring evening."

"It isn't Claire's party," she confessed, walking to the window to look down on the rose garden so that she wouldn't have to see his face when she announced her failure. "It's the car. I've reached an insurmountable obstacle."

"I don't believe it." Turning her around, he regarded her with mock horror. "This can't be my Kate. Next you'll be telling me you've decided to learn how to play bridge and are practicing balancing tea cups on your head. And what am I to tell the gardener? He's not going to be happy about having to take out the center of the rose garden so that we can have the Jaguar converted into a fountain to appease Claire's friends."

She scowled at him. "This isn't a joking matter!" she said, frustration adding a fierceness to her words.

His expression was immediately serious. "Then we'd better take a look at the situation."

"Looking at it won't help." She sighed resignedly. "A new piece, the only one I could find that might possibly work, won't fit into place, and even if it did, I can't get the timing synchronized."

Grabbing her by the arm, he half dragged her out of the room and down the hall. "A Langston never gives up without a fight to the death."

She was tempted to remind him she was only a temporary Langston, but the words refused to form. Instead she said curtly, "We fought and the Jaguar won."

"That was only round one," he countered as they continued down the stairs and out the front door.

Realizing that protesting wasn't going to do any good, she clamped her mouth shut and accompanied him in stoic silence.

When they entered the garage, he switched on the light and frowned at the assortment of tools left spread out along the fender and on the front seat. "Put on your coveralls," he ordered, taking off his jacket and tossing it onto the BMW. "Then you can show me the new piece that won't fit."

Grudgingly she obeyed.

"Now where is this piece supposed to go?" he asked, examining the uncooperative part.

"There," she said, pointing to an exposed section of the engine.

"Like this?" He frowned, attempting to insert the part upside down.

"No, like this." She took the part from him, turned it around and showed him the proper position. "But it won't work."

"Of course it will. If other people can rebuild these old cars, then so can you," he stated without reservation. "You start thinking of something inventive, and I'll phone down to the house for dinner."

While she stared at him in disbelief, he picked up the garage phone and called the kitchen. "And bring the hors d'oeuvres and champagne immediately," he finished. "We need nourishment right away."

So, sipping on chilled champagne and nibbling on caviar fed to her by Tyler, she settled back to work on the car.

Four courses and two glasses of champagne later, the part was in place and the timing was synchronized.

"Now that you've shown that engine who's boss, I think it's time to call it a night," Tyler announced as she laid aside her wrench and took a bite of chocolate mousse.

She nodded in agreement, but her smile turned into a frown as she looked at him more closely. Grease was smeared liberally on his shirt and suit pants. "Your clothes are ruined," she said in dismay.

"What are a few grease stains when rescuing a damsel in distress?" He shrugged and tossed her a playful wink.

"My knight in shining armor," she bantered lightly, covering the sudden, sharply painful wish that he honestly did consider himself her "knight."

Tyler gently caught her chin and tilted her face up to meet his steady gaze. "My armor might not be shining, but whenever you have a use for a slightly tarnished champion, remember that I'm available."

A seriousness in the dark depths of his eyes had caused her heart to skip a beat.

"I must say you've worked a miracle," Claire said, interrupting Kate's reminiscences and coming out of the house to join her. "I never believed you could get that thing running, much less create a car that any of my friends would envy."

"Thanks." Kate smiled, noting that Claire had mellowed during the past months, and though they were still not friends, the sniping had almost stopped, making life a great deal easier.

"It's a shame Tyler isn't here to break a bottle of champagne over the hood, or something to that effect," Claire mused as she continued to regard the car with interest.

"Yes, it is," Kate agreed regretfully.

Tyler had flown to Texas three weeks earlier. Ross had suddenly decided to become the manager of a rock band he had met during his nightclubbing escapades in Houston and had handed in his resignation. With his departure, the organizational mess he had created at the Houston offices of Langston Industries became painfully evident, and Tyler had been forced to fly out to straighten out the chaos and decide who could best take his brother's place. The job wasn't easy. Ross had promoted people on the basis of personal likes and dislikes with no consideration for their abilities. As a result, a great deal of sorting and shuffling of personnel had to be done, and the process that Tyler had hoped would be finished in two weeks had lengthened into three.

Although she tried not to, Kate missed him terribly. She had told herself that this was necessary practice for when they parted for good, but the thought only brought on a bout of depression. When he had called to say that he would have to stay the extra week, she'd hoped fervently that he would ask her to fly out and join him. But he hadn't. "I'm in meetings from dawn to midnight," he'd complained tiredly. She'd cautioned him not to work too hard and had forced herself to be satisfied with the two dozen roses he sent the next day.

"However," Claire went on now, "he is due in this afternoon. I know that William is supposed to meet him at the airport, but why don't you go instead in your Jaguar and surprise him?"

"That's a wonderful idea!" With an excited smile at Claire, Kate hurried toward the garage to get directions from William regarding the location of the Langston hangar.

A little before one-fifteen she parked near the side door of the hangar to which the small company jet would taxi. Her heart was pounding wildly as the sleek white two-engine plane landed and moved gracefully toward her.

Unable to control her desire to see Tyler as soon as possible, she walked quickly toward the plane as it came to a halt. The door was opened and the steps lowered and—

But it wasn't Tyler who was the first to make an appearance. It was a woman with flaming red hair. It was Linda McGreggor.

"Thank you so much, Tyler," she was saying over her shoulder. Then, pausing in the doorway of the plane, she turned back so that she could face Tyler as she added in warmly seductive tones, "I'm so glad you were able to arrange to remain an extra week."

Kate's stomach knotted. She didn't wait to hear any more. Running back to the Jaguar, she heard Tyler call her name. She started the engine, not pausing to look back, and sped from the hangar area as if she was running from the devil himself.

She didn't know where she was going. She only knew she wasn't returning to Langston Hall. During her life, she had suffered a lot of pain, but nothing had ever hurt like this. She felt betrayed and humiliated.

"It's your own stupid fault," she muttered, as she turned north onto the interstate. Forcing herself to face the truth, she admitted that, in spite of all of her efforts to the contrary, she had begun to believe that Tyler was learning to care for her. "But it was all just an act for his father," she said aloud, as if confessing her naïveté to the world would lessen the hurt. But it didn't.

Nancy had warned her. Nancy had told her how his childhood promise had become his way of life—that he never allowed himself to become too emotionally attached to anyone.

Even Claire had clearly pointed out that Tyler's work was his only real interest.

The image of Linda coming out of the plane filled Kate's inner vision. Her knuckles whitened on the wheel as she recalled Tyler's saying that Linda turned to him when she was bored. "Obviously the situation works both ways," Kate muttered grimly, forcing herself to face the full reality.

She had been an idiot to think for even a moment that someone as unsophisticated and dull as herself could hold a man like Tyler Langston for long.

Hot, angry tears burned at the back of her eyes, but she refused to cry. She had been foolish enough to forget that what she and Tyler had was strictly a business agreement. She would not compound her ridiculous flight of fancy by crying over it.

"I'M SORRY, TYLER," Linda said in apology as her driver parked in front of Langston Hall and Tyler prepared to leave the car.

"I hope you'll act with more prudence in the future," he returned coldly, then slamming out of the car, he mounted the steps two at a time.

"I wouldn't want to be in Claire's shoes," Linda said aloud to herself as she watched him go. Then, as her driver returned to the car after depositing Tyler's luggage in the front hall, she said, "Let's get out of here, James, before the fireworks start."

Inside Langston Hall, Tyler rushed in and out of rooms in search of Kate. "Damn," he muttered, when he discovered that she wasn't there.

Descending the stairs at the same angry pace at which he had ascended them, he stormed into the living room to find Claire lounging on the couch with her usual glass of wine in her hand.

"Tyler, welcome home," she purred sweetly, raising her glass in his direction.

Coming to a halt a few feet into the room, he stood with his hands on his hips and glared threateningly at his sister. "Where's Kate?"

"She's your wife. You're supposed to keep track of her, not me," Claire replied with schooled innocence.

"Don't play games with me," he warned, his expression dangerous. "Linda told me about your little scheme."

Claire's mildly drunken manner disappeared as she faced her brother with level clarity. "All's fair in war and business, my dear brother, and this time I have actually won a battle."

"And you didn't care about who you hurt in the process," he accused.

"Don't try playing the part of the noble humanitarian with me," she snapped. "Before you went off to Maine to meet Mrs. Kate Riley, I overheard you and Father arguing about his wanting you to marry her. It was too interesting an exchange not to eavesdrop on. And even rather flattering when the two of you decided to use the duration of my marriage as a time frame."

"And so from the moment Kate entered this house as my wife, you have been working to break up our marriage," Tyler snarled.

"It wasn't as if you and Kate married because you were in love," Claire pointed out. "While I realize you are capable of sweeping a woman off her feet, I did some checking and concluded that Kate wasn't a romantic victory. You spent a great deal of money on her family and set up a checking account for her before the marriage even took place. Therefore I felt it was safe to assume you'd made a deal with her. But just to be certain, I played a little game of pool with her soon after her arrival, and when I made a crack about 'bought' wives, she turned sheet white. So, given the situation, I concluded that your marriage was fair game.''

"This is no game," he snapped. "You were playing with people's lives."

Claire's eyes rounded in mock innocence. "I was merely emulating my big brother and my father."

Tyler's jaw tightened. After a moment of icy silence he said grimly, "You're right. I guess you were." With that, he abruptly left the living room.

Upstairs in his study, Tyler punched in a number on the phone. "Get me Harvey Stone," he said without preamble when someone answered.

Within a minute, Harvey was on the line.

"Kate and I had a family spat," Tyler explained coolly. "She's driving a white vintage Jaguar sports car with Massachusetts plates. I want her found, but I don't want her to know she's been found. As soon as you have any word on her, call me immediately here at my home."

KATE DROVE FOR HOURS, stopping only for gas. Night came, and the balmy weather she had left in Boston turned to the chill of a Maine November as she followed the coastline north. Earlier, she had dressed carefully to please Tyler, but the cranberry silk blouse and light wool of the jacket and skirt were no protection against the biting wind. Still, she was oblivious to physical discomfort. She was acting on a compulsion too strong to deny.

The night was clear, filled with thousands of stars, as she turned off the main road onto a side road. She didn't notice the celestial beauty and was grateful only for the full moon that lit her way as she pulled over to the side of the road and left the car. She made her way over the rocks to the small stretch of beach where her involvement with Tyler had begun.

She wasn't certain why she had come back here to this spot. Maybe it was an inner hope that if she came back to where it had all begun, she could magically lessen the hurt of the ending. Or maybe forcing herself to relive that fateful evening was the last step in facing the full extent of her foolishness.

The ocean pounded against the rocks around her, its frigid salty spray dampening her clothing and moistening her hair and face. How well she recalled her seduction of Tyler, and then his coolly delivered business offer. She shivered and pulled the lightweight jacket more tightly around her, her numb hands working clumsily. She knew she should be leaving, but the chill within her made her feel a strange kinship with the cold dark night, and she continued to stand motionless, surrounded by the sounds of an angry ocean.

Slowly another sound began to register on her senses. It was the whirring of a helicopter. Suddenly the darkness enclosing her was shattered by the beam of a strong spotlight.

Reacting to the harsh beam, she backed into a crevice.

The light was switched off, returning her shroud of darkness, but her kinship with the night had been broken. Tensely she stood, waiting for the inevitable. There was no doubt in her mind that Tyler was in that helicopter.

She heard the aircraft maneuvering inland. After a while, she saw Tyler coming toward her over the rocks, the strong beam of a flashlight illuminating his way.

"Put this on," he ordered, taking off the heavy coat he was wearing as he reached her.

"I don't want anything from you," she snarled. "I just want you out of my life."

He regarded her with concern. "You can't stay here. It's freezing, and you're already wet from the ocean spray."

She knew she wasn't behaving rationally, but she couldn't think. She was acting on raw emotion. Her hands came up defensively in front of her and she stepped back. "Stay away from me," she warned.

"What are you trying to do?" he growled, coming close again. "Are you planning to imitate Toby and catch pneumonia and die?"

Die? The thought shot through her consciousness, snapping her out of her physically withdrawn state, allowing her to realize just how cold she was. To die because she had been hurt would be the ultimate act of foolishness. "No," she answered bleakly, and leaving the crevice, passed him and scrambled up the rocks toward the waiting Jaguar.

But Tyler was right behind her, and as she reached level ground he caught her by the arm.

"Let go of me," she hissed, turning to strike at him with her free hand.

But he caught her wrist and held her captive in front of him. "You are coming back with me."

A barely decipherable "no" came out of her mouth as the cold pervaded every inch of her, causing her teeth to chatter uncontrollably and her body to shake.

"We'll continue this somewhere warm," he stated, wrapping his coat around her and lifting her into his arms.

The helicopter, which had been hovering overhead, landed again and Harvey Stone climbed out. "Need some help, Mr. Langston?" he asked.

"You can drive the Jaguar back to Boston," Tyler ordered. "The keys are still in the ignition."

"Yes, sir," Harvey said with a nod. Then glancing toward Kate, pale and angry in Tyler's arms, he added a polite "Good evening, Mrs. Langston" and headed toward the car.

Inside the helicopter, Tyler wrapped Kate in blankets until she felt like a caterpillar in a cocoon. Then, buckling her securely in the seat beside him, he ordered the pilot to take off.

As warmth returned to her body, embarrassment about her behavior grew. She had acted with self-destructive weakness, allowing emotions to rule her actions. Recalling Tyler's stated disapproval of that type of conduct made her feel even more foolish.

The sound made by the helicopter prohibited talking, a fact for which she was grateful. She wanted time to regain her balance. She wanted to be in control and coherent when she talked to Tyler.

As they flew through the night, she avoided looking at him. She knew there would be either scorn or pity in his eyes, and she was in no mood for either.

It seemed an eternity before the helicopter hovered in preparation for landing. As it began its descent, Kate peered in puzzlement at the wooded estate lit by the aircraft's powerful beam below. It wasn't Langston Hall. There was no formal rose garden in the back, and the house was a three-story square brick dwelling with no wings.

After climbing out of the helicopter when it landed on the large back lawn, Tyler lifted Kate out. Once free of the threat of the blades, he hoisted her blanket-wrapped body over his shoulder and signaled for the pilot to leave. As the aircraft began its ascent, he carried Kate toward the house.

"Put me down!" she demanded, attempting to wiggle out of his grasp, but was too tightly bundled to put up much of a struggle.

"It's supposed to be good luck for a husband to carry his wife over the threshold," he growled back, "so hold still. I would hate to drop you at this auspicious moment."

"I'm not your wife any longer," she snarled. "You were the one who made such a strong point about fidelity being a part of our agreement, and you haven't lived up to it!"

"Oh yes I have," he said angrily, as he entered the house and continued past a couple of unfurnished rooms to a wide curved staircase. "In spite of what that little scene at the airport implied, I did not spend any time with Linda in Houston. She showed up at the airport about the time my plane was getting ready for departure and asked for a ride home."

"How convenient," Kate muttered dryly, refusing to be taken in by any more of his lies.

"Convenience had nothing to do with it," he said, carrying her up the stairs and down a corridor lined with more unfurnished rooms. "It was Claire's doing. It seems she overheard my father insisting that I marry you. Then she found out about the money I had spent on your family, and putting two and two together, concluded that you and I had struck some sort of a bargain. Therefore, she reasoned that it was fair game for her to try to break up our marriage. She told Linda that I'd married you on a whim."

His scowl deepening, he corrected the statement. "Actually, she told Linda that I had an attack of acute lust mingled with male ego and that I decided I had to have you, even if it meant marrying you. Linda likes to believe that all males are especially weak on those two points, so she bought the story. Then Claire told her that I now realized what a terrible mistake I'd made but that I felt honor bound to try to make a go of the marriage. Claire said she wanted to help me and that it had occurred to her that if you were to become jealous and leave me, then I could use that as a way out and would probably take it. She convinced Linda that it was, at least, worth a try since I was so miserable. So Linda, thinking she was doing me a favor, staged that bit of playacting for you this afternoon.''

By the time Tyler finished his explanation, they had entered a furnished master bedroom, and he unceremoniously dumped Kate on the bed.

Staring at him, she fought for something to say. If what he had told her was the truth, then she had made a complete fool of herself. Even more distressing, it was obvious he expected her to continue with their arrangement. Unbundling herself from the cocoon of blankets, she caught her reflection in the dresser mirror and cringed. Her hair was a tangled mass of waves and curls, her complexion was paper white and her suit looked as if she had slept in it. "Where are we?" she asked. It was an irrelevant question at this point, but she wasn't quite ready to deal with the relevant questions just yet. She needed a few more minutes to regain control.

"We are in our home," he said levelly.

"You and I both know there has never really been an *our*," she pointed out as she fought to keep the catch out of her voice. Then, swallowing back the lump of pride that threatened to block her throat, she said, "I can't stay. You must realize that now. I care too much about you. I've tried not to care, but I do." An ironic smile flickered momentarily at one corner of her mouth. "That should give your male ego a boost." Then her voice took on a pleading quality as she met his steady gaze. "I don't want you to lose this chance for control of Langston Industries, but there must be some other way."

"There is and I've already taken it," he said gruffly.

It was over! That was what she had wanted. Still, it hurt worse than she'd ever thought anything could hurt. Afraid that he might see the sudden tears blurring her vision, she dropped her gaze to the floor.

"I have given up all of my connections with Langston Industries," he continued. "I have resigned from my position there and have offered my father first chance to buy the voting shares I've accumulated over the years."

"I—I'm sorry," she managed.

"No, I'm the one who's sorry." Gently combing the wayward strands of hair from her face with the tips of his fingers, he said with deep regret, "I'm like the greedy little boy who wanted to have his cake and eat it too."

"I know that Langston Industries means a lot to you," she murmured, pride insisting she back away from his touch. She didn't want his pity. Still, she could not force herself to give up this last fleeting feel of him. *Fool,* she called herself.

"Not nearly as much as you mean to me." Cupping her face in his hands, he tilted it upward to meet the urgent pleading in his eyes. "I love you, Kate. Please, stay with me and make this house *our* home."

Tears began to trickle down her cheeks. She wanted so much to believe him. "Knights, even those in slightly tarnished armor, aren't supposed to lie," she said shakily.

Softly his lips brushed her wet cheeks. Then, drawing her into his arms, he crushed her to him as if afraid she might try to run away again. "It's not a lie. It just took me a long time to admit it, even to myself." He paused and shook his head in self-reproach. "I should have known from the beginning. I went to Maine to find a way to convince my father that his demand that I marry you was absurd and ended up forcing you into a marriage—not because my father wanted it, but because I wanted it. All that week before the ceremony, I told myself I was acting irrationally. But I couldn't get the feel of you out of my mind nor the way those gray eyes of yours sparked when you were angry. I told myself it was a selfish wanting and I disliked myself for going through with the marriage, but I went through with it anyway. Then I discovered that I was jealous of your former husband, because you had loved him so much you were willing to seduce a stranger to keep his secret. But it wasn't until I let jealousy cause me to lose my temper over some innocent time you'd spent with William that I realized the extent of my feelings toward you. I love you and I need you, Kate. I never thought I'd say that to anyone, but it's the truth. I bought this house because I wanted us to have a life together. I had planned to bring you here as soon as I came back from Houston. I've had only the essential rooms furnished and was going to let you decorate the rest at your leisure.''

His embrace and his words were intoxicating. She wanted to lose herself in his warmth, but a nagging question persisted. "If you've given up your ties with Langston Industries, how can we afford to stay here?''

"Because, contrary to popular belief, my dear,'' he said, "Langston Industries hasn't been my only interest in life.'' He smiled crookedly. "My mother was a very wealthy woman in her own right, and when she died, she left large trusts for me, my brother and my sister. When I came into the trust, I invested the money in real estate, small companies I thought showed promise and various other ventures, many of which have proved to be very profitable.'' Kissing her on the tip of her nose, he added, "So, I can continue to support you in the fashion to which you have become accustomed.''

Her eyes glistened as the uncertainty that had haunted them vanished completely. He loved her and he needed her! She wanted to laugh and cry at the same time. But instead she asked shakily, "Does this place have a garage?''

"A very well-equipped one,'' he assured her. "I had William make certain of that.''

"In that case," she said, wrapping her arms around his neck and letting herself drown in the dark depths of his eyes, "wild horses couldn't drag me away. After all, what more could a girl want?"

"It's a bit shattering to my ego to know I'm being loved for my garage," he growled, nipping her earlobe admonishingly.

"The garage is only secondary," she whispered.

MUCH LATER, as he lay beside her, Kate leaned on an elbow and leisurely traced the line of his jaw. She felt a contentment she had never dreamed was possible. "How did you know where I would go this afternoon?" she asked softly. "I didn't even know where I was going until I got there."

"I didn't at first," he answered. "Harvey Stone had his people get on the CB airwaves and start asking truckers if they'd seen a woman driving a white vintage Jaguar sports car with Massachusetts plates. There aren't too many cars matching that description, and it didn't take long for someone to report seeing you. Once I knew what direction you were taking, it occurred to me where you might be going."

"I'm so glad you found me," she murmured huskily, kissing the corners of his mouth.

"Because I have such a wonderfully equipped garage." He frowned teasingly.

Her expression became suddenly serious as she looked hard into the soft brown depths of his eyes. "Because I love you."

"It's about time you said that, lady," he growled, his arms closing around her possessively.

The ringing of the phone woke them the next morning.

"I knew I should have waited a few days before I had that thing installed," Tyler groaned as Kate rolled out of his arms and picked up the receiver.

After a few minutes of a conversation that had been monosyllabic on her end, Kate said, "I'll speak to him." Then after adding goodbye, she hung up.

"You'll talk to whom about what?" Tyler asked, kissing her shoulder and turning her to face him.

"To you about returning to Langston Industries," she answered, her expression serious. "That was your father and he wants you back. He says he's willing to agree to any terms, within reason, that you might want. He says he doesn't want to find himself in competition with you in the marketplace."

"He can't have me back," Tyler stated. "I won't do anything that could mean risking losing you."

"You can't lose me now," she assured him, adding playfully, "Where else could I find a husband with such a well-equipped garage?"

Laughing, he started to draw her into his arms, only to be interrupted by the doorbell echoing deafeningly through the mostly unfurnished house.

"It's your turn," Kate said, pulling the covers tightly around her. "I answered the phone."

With a teasing "I'll have my revenge when I return" look, he climbed out of bed and, pulling on his pants, went downstairs as the doorbell echoed through the house again.

When Tyler returned to the room a few minutes later, he tossed a long white box onto the bed beside her. "It was for you," he growled with mock annoyance.

Opening the card and then the box, which contained a dozen long-stemmed white roses, Kate shook her head, then laughed.

"Are you going to tell me who is sending my wife flowers at this hour of the morning?" Tyler demanded.

"They're from Claire," Kate answered. "She says she's sorry for all the trouble she caused and wants to know if I'll restore a vintage Mercedes for her."

"Well?" he asked, regarding her with a grin. "What do you plan to tell her about her car?"

"I'll have to think about it." Tossing the covers off, Kate found his shirt and put it on. "And to do that I need nourishment. Is there anything to eat in this place?"

"The refrigerator is fully stocked. I had Nancy see to that yesterday," he said. As he placed a kiss on her nose, he added, "I'd never want it said that I didn't satisfy all of my wife's hungers."

"Never," she assured him.

# Harlequin Presents

## Coming Next Month

# CLAIM THE Crown

## Carla Neggers

### The complications only begin when they mysteriously inherit a family fortune.

Ashley and David. The sister and brother are satisfied that their anonymous gift is legitimate until someone else becomes interested in it, and they soon discover a past they didn't know existed.

---

# PATRICIA MATTHEWS

America's First Lady of Romance upholds her long standing reputation as a bestselling romance novelist with . . .

Caught in the steamy heat of America's New South, Rebecca Trenton finds herself torn between two brothers—she yearns for one but a dark secret binds her to the other.

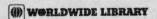

# Can you keep a secret?

## You can keep this one plus 4 free novels

# ATTRACTIVE, SPACE SAVING BOOK RACK

Display your most prized novels on this handsome and sturdy book rack. The hand-rubbed walnut finish will blend into your library decor with quiet elegance, providing a practical organizer for your favorite hard-or soft-covered books.

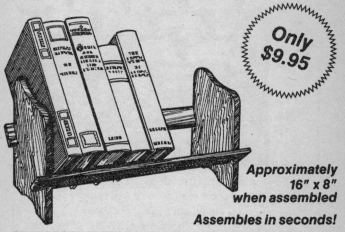

**Only $9.95**

**Approximately
16" x 8"
when assembled**

**Assembles in seconds!**

---

To order, rush your name, address and zip code, along with a check or money order for $10.70* ($9.95 plus 75¢ postage and handling) payable to *Harlequin Reader Service*:

Harlequin Reader Service
Book Rack Offer
901 Fuhrmann Blvd.
P.O. Box 1325
Buffalo, NY 14269-1325

*Offer not available in Canada.*

*New York residents add appropriate sales tax.

BKR-1R

**For the millions who can't read
Give the Gift of Literacy**

One out of five adults in North America
cannot read or write well enough
to fill out a job application
or understand the directions on a bottle of medicine.

**You can change all this by joining the fight
against illiteracy.**

For more information write to:
Contact, Box 81826, Lincoln, Neb. 68501
In the United States, call toll free: 800-228-3225

**The only degree you need
is a degree of caring**